Matt closed the distan̶ ̶ ̶ ̶e̶m̶.̶

"Afraid of what you're feeling?"

"I'm not afraid of anything. Now back off and stop trying to seduce me."

He reached out and smoothed her hair from her face before dropping his hand. "I'm not trying to seduce you. When I seduce you, you'll know it." He stepped back and spread his arms wide. "Now, where do you want me?"

Why did he keep phrasing it like that?

Rachel nodded toward the hallway. "Let's start in your office. We'll do some professional shots."

"What about the waterfall?"

A photo of this rich, gorgeous oil tycoon posing in front of a waterfall...yup, that would certainly have all the ladies drooling. Not her, of course, but the others who were bidding.

"You may just decide to bid on me yet," he drawled.

"And I prefer to leave our friendship intact, so keep those lips to yourself."

"Whatever you want," he murmured as she passed by. But his low, seductive tone indicated she wanted something else entirely and, damn it, he was right.

* * *

Most Eligible Texan is part of the Texas Cattleman's Club: Bachelor Auction series.

Dear Reader,

Who doesn't love the Texas Cattleman's Club series? I mean, come on. This ongoing story line is absolutely amazing as a reader. And as an author? I admit I get a little giddy when I'm asked to do another.

Matt and Rachel have a special history—and by special, I mean Matt has the hots for his late best friend's wife. When Rachel asks him to be part of the bachelor auction, he agrees...secretly hoping she'll be his highest bidder.

Single mom Rachel is trying to get her life back together since the death of her husband. What she doesn't have time for is unwanted passion toward her best friend. He's just been named one of the most eligible bachelors in Texas, so why would he ever be interested in someone who doesn't have a steady job and is raising a baby?

Friends to lovers is one of my absolute favorite tropes. Throw in the late husband/best friend story and I'm skipping my way from chapter one to the end!

I hope you all enjoy Matt and Rachel as much as I do!

Jules

JULES BENNETT

MOST ELIGIBLE TEXAN

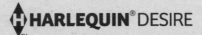

Special thanks and acknowledgment are given to Jules Bennett for her contribution to the Texas Cattleman's Club: Bachelor Auction miniseries.

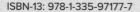

Recycling programs for this product may not exist in your area.

ISBN-13: 978-1-335-97177-7

Most Eligible Texan

Copyright © 2018 by Harlequin Books S.A.

HARLEQUIN®

www.Harlequin.com

Printed in U.S.A.

USA TODAY bestselling author Jules Bennett has published over sixty books and never tires of writing happy endings. Writing strong heroines and alpha heroes is Jules's favorite way to spend her workdays. Jules hosts weekly contests on her Facebook fan page and loves chatting with readers on Twitter, Facebook and via email through her website. Stay up-to-date by signing up for her newsletter at julesbennett.com.

Books by Jules Bennett

Harlequin Desire

What the Prince Wants
A Royal Amnesia Scandal
Maid for a Magnate
His Secret Baby Bombshell
Best Man Under the Mistletoe

Mafia Moguls

Trapped with the Tycoon
From Friend to Fake Fiancé
Holiday Baby Scandal
The Heir's Unexpected Baby

The Rancher's Heirs

Twin Secrets
Claimed by the Rancher
Taming the Texan

Texas Cattleman's Club: Bachelor Auction

Most Eligible Texan

Visit her Author Profile page at Harlequin.com, or julesbennett.com, for more titles.

To single parents trying to push through
from one day to the next.
You are somebody's hero and you've got this!

* * *

Don't miss a single book in the
Texas Cattleman's Club: Bachelor Auction
series!

Runaway Temptation
by *USA TODAY* bestselling author
Maureen Child

Most Eligible Texan
by *USA TODAY* bestselling author
Jules Bennett

Million Dollar Baby
by *USA TODAY* bestselling author
Janice Maynard
(available November 2018)

His Until Midnight
by Reese Ryan
(available December 2018)

The Rancher's Bargain
by Joanne Rock
(available January 2019)

Lone Star Reunion
by Joss Wood
(available February 2019)

One

An entire morning of pleasure reading plus an extra-large pumpkin-spice latte with a healthy dose of whip? Hell yes, sign her up.

Rachel Kincaid spotted The Daily Grind across the street and nearly skipped to the door. She had two weeks before she had to dive back into her textbooks and this was her first time out alone since giving birth eleven months ago.

Part of her felt guilty for leaving her precious Ellie, but on the other hand, she knew her baby was in the best hands back at the Lone Wolf Ranch under the care of her friend, Alexis Slade, and the host of staff members they had. The chef had taken quite a liking to Ellie and was always fussing over her.

Alexis had graciously invited Rachel and Ellie to

stay in her Royal, Texas, home and Rachel desperately needed the gal-pal time. Alexis and her grandfather Gus had gone out of their way to make the two of them feel like part of the family.

Rachel stepped up onto the curb and pulled her cell from her boho-style bag. She'd just shoot off one quick text to make sure everything was okay. Although she was most definitely looking forward to this break, she was still a fairly new mom and a bit of a worrier when it came to her baby girl.

Just as she pulled up the text messages, Rachel plowed into the door.

No, not a door. A man. A broad, strong, chiseled man.

Large hands gripped her biceps, preventing her from stumbling backward. Rachel jerked her gaze up at the stranger she'd slammed into.

Familiar dark blue eyes stared back at her, no doubt mirroring her own shock.

"Matt?"

"Rachel?"

The last time she'd been in Matt Galloway's arms had been at Billy's funeral, and that had been just over a year ago. Other than a handful of texts immediately following, she hadn't heard a word from her late husband's best friend.

The pain from the void thudded in her chest. Matt had been her friend, too, and she'd wondered where he'd disappeared to. Why he'd dodged her for so long.

"What are you doing in Royal?" she asked, pushing aside the heartbreaking thoughts.

Last she knew he was still in Dallas making millions and flashing that high-voltage smile to charm the ladies.

Matt released her and stepped back.

"Hiding out," he stated with a laugh. "I'm taking a break from the city for a bit and staying out of the limelight."

Rachel couldn't help but smile. "Ah, yes. I recall you being dubbed Most Eligible Bachelor in Texas. What's wrong, Matt? Don't want all the ladies chasing you anymore?"

Matt never minded the attention he received from beautiful women. In fact, Rachel had been interested in him at one time, but then Billy had asked her out, whisked her off her feet and, well…that was all in the past. She was moving forward now.

"Come in," he said, gesturing toward the door. "I'll buy you a cup of coffee."

"Just like that? As if the past year of silence hadn't happened?"

The words escaped her before she could stop herself. But damn it, she'd needed him and he'd vanished. Didn't she deserve to know why?

Honestly, such a heavy topic was just too much to handle this early in the morning running on little sleep and no caffeine.

"You know, never mind," she amended, waving her hand through the air as if she could just erase the words. "It's good to see you again, Matt."

She wasn't sure what to feel or what memory from

their past to cling to, as there were a great many. From meeting him and Billy for the first time at a college party, to the fun times they all had together, to the tragic death that had forever changed the dynamics between them.

Rachel pasted a smile on her face, though. She needed a day out, and running into Matt might just be what the doctor ordered. Even though he'd hurt her, she'd missed him, and she knew Matt well enough to know he had a reason for staying away. She just couldn't fathom what could keep him at such a distance for so long.

"I don't do coffee," she stated as she passed him to enter The Daily Grind. "But you can buy my glorified milkshake."

Matt placed a hand on the small of her back, a simple gesture, but one that had her inwardly cringing. Not because she didn't want Matt to touch her, but because the electric tingle that spread through her was so unexpected. No other man had touched her in so long…

She wasn't affected by him, she told herself. He was her friend, for pity's sake. No, the reaction only came from seeing him again and the lack of human contact…the lack of *male* contact.

Ugh. This was so silly. Why was she letting such a simple gesture from Matt occupy so much of her mind?

"You're going to get something pumpkin-spice with whip, aren't you?"

Rachel smacked his chest as she made her way

toward the counter. "Listen, I won't judge you and you won't judge me. Got it, Mr. Eligible Bachelor?"

Matt shook his head as he placed his order for a boring black coffee. Once Rachel placed her own order, the two of them found one of the cozy leather sofas in front of the floor-to-ceiling glass window.

The shop wasn't too busy this morning. A few people sat on stools along the back brick wall, and the bar top that stretched along the brick had power stations, so those working had taken up real estate there.

Even though they were seated in the front of the coffee shop, Rachel and Matt had just enough privacy for their surprising reunion. She still couldn't believe he was here in Royal. Couldn't believe how handsome and fit he still looked. Okay, fine. He was damn sexy and she'd have to be completely insane to think he'd ever be anything but. The past year had been nothing but kind to Matt, while she figured she looked exactly how she felt: haggard and homely.

Rachel eased back into the corner of her seat and smoothed her hands down her maxiskirt. She wasn't sure what to say now, how to close the time gap that had separated them for so long.

More importantly, she wasn't sure how to compartmentalize her emotions. Matt had been her friend for years, but seeing him now had her wondering why she felt…hell, she couldn't put her finger on the exact emotion.

"What are you doing in Royal?" Matt asked, resting his elbow on the back of the couch and shifting to face her. "You're not hiding from some newly appointed title by the media, too, are you?"

Leave it to Matt to fall back into their camaraderie as if nothing had changed between them over the last year. She'd circle back to his desertion later, but for now she just wanted a nice relaxing chat with her old friend.

"Afraid I'm not near as exciting as you," she stated with a smile. "I'm visiting Alexis Slade, my friend from college."

"I'm familiar with the Slade family. Are you alone?"

"If you're asking if I have a man in my life, no. I'm here with my daughter."

Matt opened his mouth, but before he could say anything, the barista delivered their orders and set them on the raw-edged table before them. Once they were alone again, Rachel reached for her favorite fall drink.

"I didn't mean to pry," Matt muttered around his coffee mug. "I don't have any right to know about your personal life anymore. How are you, though? Really."

"I'm doing well. But you're not prying. We've missed a good bit of each other's lives." She slid her lips over the straw, forcing her gaze away when his dark blue eyes landed on her mouth. "Ew, what is this?"

Rachel set her frosted cup back on the table. "That's not a pumpkin-spice latte."

Matt laughed. "Because that's not what you told them you wanted."

"Of course it is," she declared, swiping at her lips. "I always get the same thing at any coffee shop, especially in the fall. I'm a creature of habit and I'm pumpkin-spice everything."

"That I definitely recall." The corners of his eyes crinkled as he laughed. "But at the counter you ordered a large iced nutmeg with extra whip and an extra shot."

What the hell? Bumping into Matt had totally messed up her thought process. Maybe it was the strength with which he prevented her from falling on the sidewalk, or the firm hand on her back as he'd guided her in. Or maybe she could chalk this up to good old-fashioned lust because she couldn't deny that he was both sexy and charming.

And her late husband's best friend. There could be no lust. Not now. Not ever.

"I'll go get you another." He came to his feet. "Tell me exactly what you want."

"Oh, don't worry about it. I'm just not used to leaving the house alone—I guess it threw off my game."

Yeah, she'd go with the excuse that she was used to carrying a child and a heavy diaper bag. No way would she admit that Matt's touch, Matt's intense stare, had short-circuited her brain.

He pulled out his wallet. "Better tell me your order or I'll make something up. Do you really want to risk another bad drink?"

Rachel laughed. "Fine."

She rattled off her order and watched as he walked away.

Nerves curled in Rachel's belly. She shouldn't feel this nervous, but she did. At one time, Matt had meant so much to her—he still did. Yet she had no clue what to talk about and she certainly didn't want the awkward silence to settle between them.

One thing was certain, though. Matt hadn't changed one bit. He was still just as sexy, just as charismatic as ever. And he was the Most Eligible Bachelor in Texas. Interesting he came back into her life at this exact time.

Matt took his time getting Rachel's drink. He opted to wait at the counter instead of having the barista deliver it. He needed to get control of himself, of his thoughts. Because Rachel Kincaid, widow of Billy Kincaid, was the one person he'd thought of a hell of a lot over the years...and even more so this past year. Yes, he'd deserted her, but he'd had no other choice.

And now she'd want answers. Answers she deserved, but he wasn't ready to give.

He'd thought for sure the absence would get his emotions under control. He'd been hell-bent on throwing himself into his work, into a new partnership with his firm, and forging more takeovers in the hopes that he'd get over the honey-haired beauty that had starred in his every fantasy since they'd met.

Unfortunately, that hadn't been the case. Perhaps that's because he'd kept track of her. That sounded a bit stalkerish, but he'd needed to know she was alright. Needed to know if she was struggling so he could step in and help. From what Matt could tell, Billy's parents, plus his brother and his wife, had made sure Rachel had all she'd needed. Insurance money only went so far, but Billy came from a wealthy family.

Rachel had sold her Dallas home, though. She'd moved out and now she was here. So what was her next move? Did she have a plan? Was she going to return to Dallas?

Insurance money would run out at some point and so would her savings. Matt couldn't just let this go, not when she might need him. She'd be too proud to ever ask for help…all the more reason for him to keep an eye on her.

So many questions and he'd severed all rights to ask when he pushed her from his life. But for his damn sanity and out of respect for Rachel, he'd had no other choice.

Matt had known she'd had a little girl. She was a few months pregnant at the funeral and had already started showing. He recalled that slight swell against him as he'd held her by the graveside.

He'd honestly had no idea she'd be here in Royal, but like the selfish prick he was, he wasn't a bit sorry he'd run into her. Now was the time to pay his penance and admit he'd dodged her, admit that he needed space. But one thing he could never admit was his attraction. That was the last thing Rachel needed to be told.

"Here you go," the barista said with a smile as she placed the new frothy drink on the counter.

Matt nodded. "Thanks."

The second he turned back toward Rachel, the punch of lust to his gut was no less potent than it had been the first time he'd seen her all those years ago. She'd always been a striking woman, always silently demanded attention with just a flick of her wavy blond hair, a glance in his direction. Hell, all he had to do was conjure up a thought and she captivated him.

And nothing had been as gut-wrenching as watching her marry his best friend…a man who hadn't deserved someone as special as Rachel.

Rachel was, well, *everything*. But she wasn't for him.

Matt wasn't sure what was worse, staying in Dallas dodging paparazzi over this damn Most Eligible Bachelor in Texas title or being in this small town face-to-face with the one woman he could never have—the only woman he'd ever truly wanted.

A group of college-aged kids came through with their laptops and headed to the back of the coffee shop. Their laughter and banter instantly thrust him back to that party where he had first met Rachel. He'd flirted a little and was about to ask her out when

Billy slid between them and whispered, "Mine," toward Matt before whisking her away.

If only Matt had known how things would go down between Billy and Rachel...

"One extra-shot pumpkin-spice latte with a side of pumpkin and pumpkin whip on top." Matt placed the drink in front of Rachel and made a show of bowing as he extended his arm. "Or something like that."

Rachel's laughter was exactly the balm he needed in his life. "Thank you, but that wasn't necessary."

"Was the bow too much?"

He took a seat next to her and couldn't take his eyes off the way her pretty mouth covered the pointed dollop of whip or the way she licked her lips and groaned as her lids lowered. Damn vixen had no idea what she could do to a man. He wondered how many others she'd put under her spell.

"So, tell me all about this newly appointed title." She set her drink on the table and tore the paper off her straw. "Are we going to get bombarded by squealing fans or camera flashes?"

"I sure as hell hope not." Matt grabbed his mug and settled back into the corner of the sofa. "And I'd rather not discuss all of that. Let's talk about you. What are you doing here in Royal? Other than staying with the Slades."

Rachel held on to her cup and crossed her legs. The dress she wore might be long, but the thin fabric hugged her shapely thighs and shifted each time she moved. And from the way she kept squirming, she wasn't as calm as her smile led him to believe.

"I'm working on finishing my marketing degree online and figuring out where to go from here."

Matt didn't like that there was a subtle lilt leading him to believe she wasn't happy. The thought of her not moving on to a life she deserved didn't sit well with him. Not one bit.

"How much longer do you have?" he asked.

Rachel slid her fingertip over the condensation on her glass. "One more semester and I'm done. The end can't come soon enough."

And being a single mother no doubt added to her stress. Surely she wasn't strapped for cash. Her in-laws alone should've covered anything she needed that Billy's finances couldn't.

She'd been working on her degree when they'd met, but once she and Billy married, Billy had talked her out of finishing. Matt was damn proud she was doing this for herself.

He had so many questions, yet none of them he should ask just yet. Even though she smiled and laughed, he'd seen the hurt in her eyes, the accusation in her question when they'd been outside. Rachel deserved her answers well before he was allowed to have his.

Matt wasn't going to leave Royal without making sure Rachel and her daughter were stable and had what they needed, at least until she got on her feet.

Well, hell. Is that why they were here? Because

she didn't have a place to stay? What about the home she and Billy had?

"How long are you hiding from your fan club?" she asked, pulling him back to the real reason he was in town.

Matt clenched his jaw. He wasn't about to get into all the issues he had going on. The disagreements with his partner, the negotiations he had still up in the air, the fact he wanted to sell his 51 percent and start his own company. There really was no way to just sum up in a blanket statement all he had going on.

He would much rather keep their unexpected reunion on the lighter side. And now that they were both in Royal, Matt sure as hell planned to see her again. Fate had pushed them together for a reason and he couldn't ignore that.

"I'm going to be here awhile. My grandfather's old estate is on the edge of town. It's sat empty for several years. Figure I should think about having it renovated and perhaps selling. For now, I'm staying at The Bellamy."

The five-star establishment had been recently renovated into a luxurious hotel. Matt had requested the penthouse and had paid extra to have it ready on the same day he'd had his assistant call for the reservation. Money might have gotten him pretty much everything he wanted in life, but there was still a void. Something was missing and he had no clue what it was.

Rachel slid those plump lips around her straw again and Matt found himself shifting in his seat once more. He'd been in her presence for all of ten minutes and it was as if no time had passed at all. He still craved her, still found her one of the most stunning women he'd ever known. Still wondered what would've happened between them if Billy hadn't been at that party.

Actually, there wasn't a day that went by that he didn't wonder. If he were being honest, most of the women he'd hooked up with were just fillers for the one he truly wanted.

Matt set his mug on the table, then leaned closer to her. "Listen, Rachel…"

"No." She held up her hand and shook her head. "Let's not revisit the past. Not quite yet."

He stared at her for another minute, wanting to deal with the proverbial elephant in the room, and yet needing to dodge it at the same time.

Finally, he nodded. "Since we're both in town for a while, I'll treat you to dinner tonight."

Rachel laughed. "I'm not the carefree woman I used to be, Matt. I'm a single mother with responsibilities."

"Bring your daughter."

Where had that come from? He'd never asked a woman and her child on a date. Had he ever even dated a woman with a kid?

He hadn't. But none of that mattered, because no other woman was Rachel. Besides, he wanted to see Billy's daughter. His best friend might not have been the world's greatest husband, but he was a good friend and his child would be the last connection to him.

Rachel's smile widened as she reached out and gripped his hand. "It's a date."

Matt glanced down at their joined hands and wondered why he'd just jumped head first into the exact situation he'd been running from. If he stayed around Royal too long with Rachel, he didn't know how long he could resist her…or if he'd even try.

Two

"From the way you're eyeing those photos, maybe you should consider bidding on your own bachelor."

Smiling, Rachel glanced up from the glossy images all spread out across the farm-style kitchen table to look at Alexis. Each picture featured a single man in Royal who had agreed to step up to the plate and be auctioned for a good cause. All funds would go toward the Pancreatic Cancer Research Foundation, but each woman writing the check would be winning a fantasy date with one hunky bachelor.

Rachel and Alexis were still searching for someone who could be the "big draw" or headliner.

"I think I'll just stick to the marketing and working behind the scenes and not worry so much about getting my fantasy date." Rachel blew out a breath and flattened her palms on the spread of photos. She did some quick figures in her head of what she could donate and still live off of until she completed her degree and got a paying job. "Don't worry, I'll still write a check for the cause. There are so many great guys who agreed to help… I'm just not sure which one we should use as the main event."

Alexis dropped to a chair next to Rachel and started sliding the images around. She picked up one, then set it aside, picked up another, dismissed it, too. There were so many options, from doctors to lawyers, ranchers to pilots. Royal had quite the variety of upstanding men. How were all of these hotties still single?

"The problem is these guys are all fabulous," Alexis stated, her blue eyes searching all of the options. "You can't go wrong with any of them. We do need the final man to be someone spectacular, someone the ladies won't mind writing an exorbitant amount for."

A small white paper with handwritten notes was paper clipped to the top right corner of each picture. The brief stats gave basic details of the bachelor: name, age, occupation. The overwhelming response from handsome, eligible men to help with the charity auction was remarkable. The Pancreatic Cancer Research Foundation would no doubt get a fat check afterward.

Gus and Alexis had done all the grunt work lining up the bachelors and it was Rachel's job to make sure word got out and women flocked with full purses to the biggest event of the year.

"We need to get these framed," Rachel murmured, thinking aloud. "They need to be propped on easels and in sturdy wood frames to showcase all this glorious masculinity."

They'd have to strategically set them around the outdoor garden area at the Texas Cattleman's Club so the women could come early and get an idea of who they wanted to bid on. Once Rachel went to the site, she could better plan all the details of how to arrange things.

She had already made a mock-up of the programs that would be handed out at the door. The program featured the bachelors with their regular posed image, plus she'd requested something playful or something to show their true personality.

"I have a spreadsheet of the order I think they should go in," Rachel stated. "Sorry, I know that's not quite marketing, but I was up late last night and started thinking of the best way to advertise and then I started numbering them and—"

"I get it. Your OCD kicked in and you ran with it." Alexis reached for her girlfriend's hand and squeezed. "I'll take any help I can get, and having you stay here is just like being in college. Well, with a child and less parties, but I love having you at the ranch."

Rachel loved being here, as well. She had been feeling adrift, but when Alexis had invited her to

Royal, she figured this was just the break from life she needed. Who knew? Maybe Royal would become home. The big-city feel with the small-town attitude of everyone helping each other was rather nice.

Plus, there was the bonus of her best friend living here. Ellie seemed to have taken to Alexis and Gus.

"Lone Wolf Ranch is gorgeous," Rachel said, beaming. "I'm still excited you asked me to help with this auction. I think it's going to pull in more money than you ever thought possible."

Alexis pulled her hand away and blew out a sigh. "I don't know. I've set a pretty large goal. This fund-raiser means more to me than just money. I want to honor my grandmother's memory and make my grandfather proud of me at the same time. They did so much for me growing up."

Rachel knew this was so much more than a show or a popularity contest. Alexis lost her grandmother to pancreatic cancer and all of the funds from The Great Royal Bachelor Auction would go straight to the foundation in loving memory of Sarah Slade.

"She would definitely be proud of you," Rachel stated. "You're doing great work."

"I think you're doing most of it. I'd seriously be overwhelmed without you."

Rachel pulled all of the photos into a stack and neatened them up with a tap onto the table. "I'd say we make a great team."

The back door opened and Alexis's grandfather,

Gus Slade, stepped inside. He swiped the back of his arm across his forehead and blew out a whistle.

"An old man could get used to walking in his back door and seeing two beautiful ladies."

Rachel flashed him a grin. If Gus was about thirty years younger, she'd make him the headliner for the auction. The elderly widower was quite the charmer and his dashing good looks and ruggedness would make him a surefire hit. No woman could resist his thick silver hair and broad shoulders. The weathered, tanned skin and wrinkles around his blue eyes only added to his masculine appeal. Why couldn't women age as gracefully?

"Where is the youngest lady?" Gus asked as he headed to the fridge and pulled out a bottle of water.

"Ellie needed a nap," Rachel replied. "She was rather cranky."

"She's a sweetheart," Gus defended. "I get a little cranky when I need a nap, too."

Rachel's heart swelled at how easily Alexis and her grandfather just took in two stray guests as if they were all one big happy family. Rachel had only been in Royal a short time, but she already felt like this was home. She hadn't really had a sense of belonging since Billy's death. Staying in Dallas in their home hadn't felt right. Especially considering the house they'd lived in had been purchased without her approval. He'd surprised her with it and she'd never really liked the vast space. The two-story home had seemed too staid, too cold.

She'd sold that house not too long ago and moved to a small rental house, much to the shock of Billy's family. Speaking of, life had been even more stressful with her in-laws hovering and making it a point to let her know they'd be willing to keep Ellie for a while so Rachel could finish her degree.

Then Billy's brother and his wife offered to take Ellie to make Rachel's life "easier." What the hell? She didn't care about easy. She cared about her child and providing a stable future.

Ellie was the only family she had and Rachel wasn't going to be separated from her for any amount of time. She'd give up her degree first. Ellie was her world...a world Rachel hadn't even known she'd wanted until the time came.

Billy hadn't wanted children and they'd both been taken by surprise when Rachel had gotten pregnant. Rachel had slid into the idea of motherhood and couldn't imagine a greater position to be in. Billy, on the other hand, hadn't gotten used to the idea before his death. In fact, that was one of the things they'd argued about right before he'd left that fateful day.

Rachel didn't have many regrets in life, but that argument still haunted her.

"Well, I hope you both are saving your appetites for a good dinner tonight." Gus's statement pulled Rachel from her thoughts. "I've got the chef preparing the best filets with homemade mashed potatoes and her special gravy, and baby carrots fresh from the garden."

All of that sounded so amazing. Any other night Rachel would welcome all those glorious calories. In fact, she'd enjoyed each meal their chef prepared over the past several days. If she hung around much longer she'd definitely be packing on the pounds.

"I actually have plans."

Alexis and Gus both turned to her like she'd just announced her candidacy for president. Rachel couldn't help but laugh at their shocked faces.

"I ran into an old friend earlier at Daily Grind and he asked to see me tonight. I'll be taking Ellie, so don't worry. You won't be babysitting."

Alexis waved her hands and shook her head. "Hold up. Forget the babysitting, which I'd happily do. You said *he*. You're going on a date?"

Rachel cringed. "No, not a date. Matt is an old friend."

"Matt who?" Gus asked, his brows drawing inward like a concerned parent.

"Galloway."

Gus's features relaxed as he nodded. "Businessman from Dallas, also a member of TCC. So, he asked you on a date?"

"No, it's not a date," she repeated, feeling like perhaps she shouldn't have disclosed her plans.

"Matt Galloway. Oh, I remember him," Alexis murmured. "A businessman from Dallas sounds perfect. How old is he now? Early thirties, right?"

"A few years older than me. Why do you say he's perfect?"

Alexis's smile beamed and she merely stared. Then Rachel realized exactly where her friend's thoughts had traveled.

"No." Rachel shook her head and gripped the stack of photos. "We have our guys and I'm not asking my friend to do this. I couldn't. We just reconnected after a year apart and he was one of Billy's best friends. It would just be too weird."

Not to mention her heart rate still hadn't recovered from their morning together. Part of her felt guilty for the way she'd reacted. Yes, her husband was gone, but was it okay to already feel a flicker of desire for another man? And one of her friends at that. Surely her sensations were all just heightened over their reunion. Rachel was confident the next time she saw Matt it would just be like old times when they hung out as pals.

And if that attraction tried to rear its ugly head, Rachel would just have to ignore it. A romantic entanglement between the two of them was *never* going to happen. Besides, even though a chunk of time had passed, Rachel still considered Matt someone special in her life. So, no. She couldn't ask him to put himself up on the stage…especially considering he was trying to stay out of the public eye.

"You didn't tell me he was named Most Eligible Bachelor in Texas," Alexis exclaimed.

Rachel blinked and focused on her friend who had her phone in hand, waving it around. An image of Matt in a tux on the red carpet posing in front of some charitable gala had Rachel sighing.

"No, I didn't tell you that. One of the reasons why he's in Royal is to lie low."

"Rach, no guy can look like this and have women ignore him. It's not possible."

"Looks like a perfect candidate for you to bid on, Lex," Gus chimed in with a nudge to his grand-daughter. "You're putting in all this work—you should pick out a date, as well."

The idea of her best friend and her other friend hooking up hit the wrong chord in Rachel. But what could she say? She had no claims on Matt, and Alexis was single. They both could do whatever they wanted…but Rachel wasn't so sure she'd like it.

"Poor guy," Gus added, leaning over to look at the photo. "It's hell when the women are all over you and you have no place to hide. I feel his pain."

Alexis rolled her eyes and laid her phone down on the table. "Ignore him. He's a romantic. But let's focus on Matt. Seems like he's the perfect big name for our auction needs. Figured I'd look him up really quick and see how we can market him."

As if he were cattle ready to go to the market. Rachel was fine discussing the other bachelors; in fact, she rather enjoyed using her creativity and school-ing to make each guy stand out in a unique way. But something about the idea of Matt up for grabs really irritated the hell out of her.

Perhaps it was because Rachel knew for a fact that

the female attendees would bid high on the very sexy, very wealthy Matt Galloway, but she didn't want to give them the opportunity.

First, she'd feel like a jerk asking him when he'd been up-front as to his reasons for being in Royal. He was dodging this new title and clearly not comfortable with the added attention.

Second, the idea of women waving their paddles and tossing money for a fantasy date with Matt... well, she was jealous. *There.* She admitted it—if only to herself.

Why was she suddenly so territorial? She'd always found Matt attractive, always respected and admired him. How could she throw him into the lion's den, so to speak, and expect not to have strong feelings on the matter? They were friends. She should feel protective, but there were other feelings swirling around inside her, and none of them remained in the friend zone.

"Tell me you'll at least think about it."

Rachel met Alexis's pleading gaze. She was here to help her friend—they were actually helping each other—and this auction was a huge deal to the Slade family. How could Rachel say no when Alexis had opened her home and heart to Rachel and Ellie?

"I'll see what I can do," she conceded with a belabored sigh. "But I can't promise anything and I won't beg."

Alexis squealed. "All I ask is you try."

Gus rested a large, weathered hand on Alexis's

shoulder. "My granddaughter is all Slade. When she wants something, she finds a way to make it happen. So, which guy are you bidding on, Lex?"

Alexis rolled her eyes. "Stop trying to marry me off. I'm working on raising money, not finding a guy to put a ring on my finger."

Rachel scooted her chair back and came to her feet. "Well, I'm pretty determined to help bring in all the money possible, but I won't make Matt feel uncomfortable."

"I understand," Alexis said, nodding in agreement. "But, I'll wait up so I can hear all about your date and see if he agreed to be auctioned."

That naughty gleam in her friend's eyes was not going to last. If Alexis knew all that Rachel, Matt and Billy had been through, she'd understand just how delicate this situation was. But she wasn't wanting to get into all of that now. She didn't want to revisit the ordeal that was her marriage and the gap of time she'd missed Matt.

"Feel free to wait up, but I assure you I won't be out long. I have a baby, remember? Early bedtimes are a must."

"Why don't you leave her here?" Gus suggested. "It's nice having a little one around, and she's no trouble."

Alexis stood up and patted her grandfather's shoulder. "If that's a hint, relax. It's going to be a while before I give you a great-grandchild. I'm a little busy in case you haven't noticed."

Rachel didn't miss the way Alexis's eyes landed on the top photo…which featured the very handsome Daniel Clayton.

Alexis Slade and Daniel Clayton had once been quite an item, but they'd fallen apart and Rachel still didn't know what had happened. Whenever Rachel brought up the topic, her friend not-so-subtly steered their chat in another direction. Eventually, Rachel would find out what was going on between her friend and the mysterious ex.

"What time is your date?" Alexis asked.

Resigned to the fact nobody believed her about the nondate, Rachel shrugged. "We kept it open. He realizes I need to be flexible with a little one. I'll head over to his hotel room later. Once Ellie wakes, I need to grab a shower and we both need to get ready."

"What are you taking?" Alexis asked.

"Taking?"

"A bottle of wine? A dessert? I'm sure we have something the cook has whipped up. She always has breads."

Rachel shook her head. "I'm not taking anything. You're letting that romantic streak show."

"Just trying to help," she muttered.

Rachel patted her friend's arm. "I know, but I've only been a widow for a year. I'm not ready to rush into anything."

Her marriage had started out in a whirlwind of lust and stars in their eyes. Rachel and Billy had lived life to the fullest and loved every minute of it. Then the pregnancy had slid between them and continued to drive a wedge through their relationship. They'd built something on top of shaky ground and hadn't realized until after the fact.

Unfortunately, Rachel would never know if their marriage would've worked itself out. Would Billy have ever settled down and stepped into the role of loyal father and devoted husband?

Pain gripped her from so many angles, but she had to keep pushing forward for her sake as well as Ellie's. Rumored infidelity and ugly arguments weren't how she wanted to remember her late husband.

"I'm going to go check on Ellie," Rachel told them. "She should be waking soon. Lex, I'll get you a list of the order I think we should use for the auction. If Matt isn't onboard, then Daniel might be our best bet as the big-name draw."

Her friend's lips thinned, her jaw clenched. Gus blew out a breath that Rachel would almost label as relief, and he had a satisfied grin. Whatever was going on with Daniel and Alexis—or wasn't going on—was quite a mystery.

One thing was certain, though—Alexis was not a fan of having Daniel up on the auction block. Ironically, Rachel still wasn't too keen on the idea of Matt being up there, either.

Because if that came to pass, one or both of them might just have to grab a paddle and place their own bids.

Three

Matt tipped the waitstaff a hefty amount for their quick, efficient service and for meeting his last-minute demands. He hadn't known what to have for dinner for Rachel, let alone an infant.

Infant? Toddler? What was the right term for an eleven-month-old? He knew nothing about children and had never taken to the notion of having his own, so he'd never bothered to learn.

But he was interested in Rachel, and she and Ellie were a package deal that he didn't mind. No matter the years that passed, no matter the fact she'd married his best friend, nothing at all had ever diminished his desire for Rachel. He'd hid it as best he could, often gritting his teeth and biting his tongue when Billy would be disrespectful to Rachel's needs.

Once Rachel got pregnant, the two started fighting more, and Billy's answer was to get out of the house so they both could cool off. Those times when Matt and Billy were at the Dallas TCC clubhouse shooting pool and drinking beer or even out on Matt's boat on the lake, Billy never did grasp that running didn't solve the problem. He never once acted excited about the pregnancy. He never mentioned how Rachel felt about being a mother. Billy's life didn't change at all and Matt knew Rachel hurt alone.

He also knew she'd been excited about the pregnancy, but how much could she actually enjoy it knowing her husband wasn't fully committed?

Whenever Matt would mention anything to Billy about Rachel, the other man always told him to mind his own business and that he didn't know what marriage was like. Valid point, but Matt knew how to treat a woman and he damn well respected Rachel.

Matt stepped back and surveyed the dinner he'd had set up on the balcony. His penthouse suite at The Bellamy had a sweeping view of the immaculate grounds, yet was private enough he felt comfortable bringing Rachel out here to talk.

He hoped this setting was okay. For some asinine reason he was a damn nervous wreck. What the hell? There had never been a woman to make him question himself or his motives. Even when he and Rachel had been friends before, the main emotion that always hovered just below the surface had always been forbidden desire.

But she was a different woman now. She was a single mother seeking out a fresh start, not some short-term fling with her late husband's best friend. And he wasn't looking for anything more than exploring the connection and seeing if this was just one-sided.

Matt needed to curb his desire. She wasn't coming here for a quickie. He'd invited her as a friend… and unfortunately, he feared that was the category she'd try to keep him in. Being near her again only put his desires right on the edge, and he had to retain control before he fell over the line of friendship and pulled her right with him.

Even now that she was single, he still had no chance with her because he was known as a ladies' man, the Most Eligible Bachelor in Texas, and Rachel was a sweetheart who wouldn't settle for anything less than happily-ever-after.

Damn that title. It had been nothing but a black cloud over him since he'd been given the title some men would happily flaunt. He was not one of those men. He hadn't even been able to go on a damn date back in Dallas without a snap of the camera or someone coming up to him asking for his autograph.

The final straw had been when he'd come home to his penthouse and a reporter was lurking outside his door. He'd fired his security guard promptly after that irritating inconvenience.

The one woman he wanted could never be his,

even temporarily. Perhaps that was his penance for lusting after his best friend's wife.

Matt looked at all the items he'd ordered. He might not know much about children, but he'd paid his assistant a nice bonus to make a few things happen within the span of a few hours and by just making some calls. Even from Dallas, the woman was working her magic here in Royal and had baby things delivered in record time. That woman definitely deserved a raise. She saved his ass on a daily basis.

With one last glance, he started having doubts. The balcony ledge went up waist-high on him, the wrought iron slats were about an inch apart. There shouldn't be a problem with Ellie out here, especially with all the other paraphernalia to keep her occupied, but seriously, what did he know about this? Did she walk or crawl? Did she look like Rachel or Billy?

Nerves pumped through him and he didn't like it. Not one bit. Matt never got nervous. He'd handled multibillion-dollar mergers and never broken a sweat, so it baffled his mind as to why he was getting all worked up.

Besides, what did he think would happen here tonight? Did he truly believe they could pick back up where they'd left off before Billy died? He'd deserted her due to his own selfish needs and worry he wouldn't be able to control those wants. He'd had to push her away for both of their sakes.

Surely he wasn't so delusional to think that she'd…what? Want to tumble into bed with him?

He'd be a complete liar if he said he hadn't fantasized about her since the moment they'd met. There was probably some special pocket of hell for men like him, coveting his best friend's wife.

But Rachel had always been different. Perhaps it was her beauty or the way his entire body tightened with desire when she was around. Maybe it was the way she could go up against anyone in a verbal sparring match that he found so sexy.

Hell, he had no idea. What he was sure of, though, was that having her come to his suite and bring her child along might have been the worst idea he'd ever had.

No, the worst idea he'd had was letting Billy ask Rachel out first. That was where Matt had gone wrong from the start.

The bell chimed throughout the suite and he raked a hand over his cropped hair as he crossed the spacious room. There was no going back now, and he wasn't about to keep second-guessing himself. Rachel was a friend; so what if he had her over for dinner?

Yet you want more.

He wished like hell the devil on his shoulder would shut up. Matt was well aware of exactly what he wanted from Rachel, but he respected her enough not to seduce her.

With a flick of the lock, Matt pulled the door open and every single best intention of keeping his thoughts platonic vanished.

The formfitting blue shirt that matched her eyes hung off one shoulder. Those well-worn jeans hugged her shapely hips, and her little white sneakers had him immediately thinking back to the younger version he'd first met. But this grown-up Rachel had a beautiful baby girl on her hip…a baby that was a mirror image of her mother right down to the prominent dimples around her mouth.

Matt had always been fascinated by Rachel's mouth and those damn dimples. Every time she smiled, he'd been mesmerized.

"Come in."

Geesh, he'd been staring and reminiscing like some hormonal teen. He was a damn grown man, CEO of a billion-dollar company, and he stood here as if he'd never seen an attractive woman before.

"Wow, this is one snazzy hotel."

Rachel moved into the living area and spun in a slow circle. Her daughter still clutched her little arms around her mother's shoulders.

"I thought the outside was impressive," she stated. "But this penthouse suite is bigger than the apartment I'd been renting."

Matt frowned. Why the hell had she lived in such a small space to begin with? He understood her emotional reasoning for selling the home she and Billy shared, but why an apartment? Could she not afford another home?

He had no right to ask about her financial standing,

but that's exactly what he wanted to do. Obviously this wasn't something he'd get into with Ellie here.

"I figure this is a good place to hide while I'm in town," he joked. "I can work from the offices at the TCC clubhouse and come back here and enjoy the amenities of the gym and sauna, and having dinner here is no hardship."

Rachel patted her daughter's back. "Then you can stay up here on the balcony and look down on the peons and paparazzi?"

"Something like that," Matt laughed. "Actually, I had our dinner set up out there if you'd like to head out. The view is breathtaking."

Rachel moved toward the open French doors. "I don't know if it's safe to have Ellie out here."

As she stepped outside, she gasped as she took in everything he'd done. "Matt, my word! What didn't you think of?"

Matt shrugged, wondering if he'd gone overboard. Hell, he hadn't known what to do, so in those instances his default was always to do everything. His motto had always been "Better to have too much than not enough."

"I wasn't sure if she used a high chair," he stated, stepping over the threshold to join her. "When I called my assistant for reinforcements, I told her to ask for the works. The guy came to set all of this up and asked how many kids I had."

Rachel laughed as she turned and surveyed the spacious balcony. Matt couldn't take his eyes off her or her daughter. He wasn't even sure how to feel looking at Billy's child, but when he saw that sweet girl, he really only saw Ellie.

Guilt slithered in slowly from so many different angles. He shouldn't still have been lusting after his late friend's wife, but there was clearly no stopping that. But he also shouldn't be wanting to get closer to Rachel knowing full well that he wasn't looking for a family or any type of long-term commitment.

Being married to a career didn't leave much time for feeding into a relationship. Besides, he couldn't lose Rachel as a friend. The risks were too high that that was exactly what would happen if he pressed on with his pent up desires.

Rachel still hadn't said anything as she continued to take in everything. One area of the stretched balcony looked as if a department store had set up their latest display of baby gear. High chair, Pack 'n Play, play mat, toys, stationary swing…

"I don't know the age for any of this stuff, so if you need something else let me know and I'll call—"

"No." Rachel turned back around to face him, her eyes filled with unshed tears. "This is… I don't even have words. You invited me for dinner and thought of everything for Ellie."

His gaze darted to the child in question. Her wide brown eyes, exactly like Rachel's, were focused on him. She clutched a little yellow blanket against her chest and huddled against her mother for security. Something shifted inside Matt, an unknown emotion he couldn't label and wasn't sure he wanted to explore.

"She's beautiful." Matt turned his gaze back to Rachel as a shimmer of awareness flowed through him. "Just like her mother."

She blinked and glanced away, never one to take a compliment. That had never stopped him from offering them. Even when the three of them had all hung out, back in the day, Matt would tell her she looked nice or he liked her hair. There hadn't been a time he recalled hearing Billy compliment his wife, and Matt hadn't been able to help himself. Billy had been a great friend, yet from everything Matt could tell, he had been a lousy husband.

But really, all of this was a moot point. Because regardless of the state of their marriage, Matt knew he shouldn't be trying to make a play for Billy's wife. He had regrets in his life, but this might be the most asshole-ish thing he'd ever done. Still, Matt had never backed away from what he wanted…and he wanted the hell out of Rachel Kincaid.

"Who else is eating with us?" Rachel asked as she stared at the spread he'd ordered.

"Just us. I ordered all of your favorites. Well, what I remember you ordering in the past, but I didn't know what you were in the mood for."

Rachel wrinkled her nose. "I'm a boring creature of habit. I pretty much stick with pizza, pasta or any other carb. This all looks amazing."

He took a step forward and offered a smile.

"You're not boring," he corrected. "There's nothing wrong with knowing what you want. I'm the same way. I see something I want, I make it mine."

Damn it. He needed to calm the hell down. Hadn't he told himself to get control over his desires?

But saying and doing were clearly two different things because he couldn't stop himself. Rachel pulled out emotions in him he couldn't even describe.

Her eyes widened. "Are you talking about food or something else?"

Matt shrugged, forcing himself to take a step back and not get her any more flustered. "We'll discuss food. For now."

Rachel moved to the Pack 'n Play and sat Ellie down. The little girl whimpered for a moment before Rachel pulled a doll from the diaper bag on her shoulder. Damn it, why hadn't he taken that from her?

"Let me help." He took the bag from her shoulder. "Damn, woman, what do you have in here?"

Rachel straightened and turned. "It's amazing how one little person can need so many things. Diapers, wipes, butt paste—"

"Pardon?"

She laughed and went on. "I have an extra change of clothes in case of blowouts, food, snacks, toys, pain reliever for her swollen gums…"

"I don't know if I want any more information about the butt paste and blowouts." Matt set the diaper bag next to the door. "I'll fix you a plate. The restaurant downstairs serves some of the best food I've ever had and I've been all around the world. I ordered their rosemary bread because when I called, they said they'd just taken it from the oven."

"Well, you clearly know me," she said with a wide smile that punched him with another dose of lust. "If it's carbs, I'm in."

"Do you still have a love for key lime pie?"

Rachel rolled her eyes. "If you mean do I still inhale it like it's my job, then yes. I don't even care about the added pounds. Key lime pie is so worth it."

"You're still just as stunning as always, Rachel. No pounds could change that."

She crossed her arms over her chest and tilted her head. "I'm starting to see why you were the recipient of the most prestigious bachelor title. You're still quite the charmer."

He might try to charm other women—well, he didn't try; he flat-out *did* charm them. But with Rachel, he wasn't trying. He always spoke the truth, always wanted her to know her value and how special she was.

If you cared so much, you wouldn't have let a year pass since seeing her.

"I've missed you," she stated, as if reading his mind. "I miss our friendship."

Friendship. Yes. That's the only label their relationship could have, because she was a widow, a single mother and she wasn't looking to jump back into anything. Honestly, he wasn't looking to fill the role of Daddy, either, but that didn't stop the fact he wanted Rachel as more than a friend.

Likely she'd thrown that out there as a reminder, but he dismissed the words. He'd respect her if she flat-out wasn't interested, but he had to know. He had to know if she was interested in him. He needed to find out if she burned for him as much as he for her. Would she even want to attempt anything physical knowing he wasn't ready for anything more?

Why did this all have to be so damn complicated? Oh, right. Because he'd spent years building and attempting to ignore these emotions.

"I'd better eat before she starts fussing," Rachel told him as she went to take a seat. "There's always a small window of opportunity and I rarely get warm food because I feed her first."

Matt urged Rachel toward the table and pulled her chair out. "If she fusses, I'm sure I can hold her and entertain her while you finish, or I can feed her. Regardless, you are eating right now while it's warm, and there will be no arguments."

Rachel looked up at him and quirked one brow. "You ready to play Uncle Matt?"

Ouch. That stung. He wasn't sure what he wanted to be called…then again, he hadn't given it much thought. He was having difficulty processing much of anything with that creamy shoulder of Rachel's on display and her familiar floral fragrance teasing his senses.

"I win over billion-dollar mergers before breakfast," he joked. "I'm pretty sure I can handle a little person."

Rachel snorted. "Don't get too cocky. It's harder than it looks."

"I never doubted that for a minute," he corrected. "Now eat. There's plenty."

Once she took a seat, Matt eased it closer to the table. He immediately started filling her plate with rosemary bread and Alfredo over penne and chicken, then filled her glass with pinot grigio.

"You put all of this together pretty quick considering you just asked me today."

Matt set her food in front of her before taking a seat across the table. "Just a few calls and the right connections. Why wouldn't I go all out for a friend I haven't seen in a year?"

Her stare leveled his. "I'd think a cup of coffee or a stroll in the park would've sufficed."

Matt reached across the table and squeezed her fingers. Her eyes immediately darted to their joined hands. "You have every right to be angry with me."

"I'm not angry," she retorted.

Matt raked his thumb across the silky ridge of her knuckles before easing back. He noticed she didn't wear her wedding band any longer and part of him swelled with approval and excitement.

"Hurt then. You can't lie to me, Rachel. Billy's death did something to both of us."

Like the fact he couldn't be the one to console her. He simply…damn it, he couldn't. He'd wanted too much for too long so he'd had to let her go and pray someone else offered the comfort she needed. Because if he'd had to hold her day after day, night after night until her pain had eased...

"I was hurt," she admitted. "I still am, actually. Care to tell me why you just disappeared?"

"I texted."

Such a lame defense, yet the words left his mouth before he could stop himself. Out of everything and everyone in his life, Rachel was the one he'd barely been able to control himself around.

"I don't really want to dredge up the past right now. I want answers from you, but let's not do it tonight." She picked up her fork and offered a typical dimpled smile. "Billy was a big part of my life, but I've worked hard at moving on. I'm trying to make a future for Ellie and me. Always looking back isn't the way to do that."

He had to hand it to her. She'd hurt from her husband's death, from Matt's absence, from being thrust into being a single mother, yet she forced herself to trudge on.

"So, you're finishing your degree," he started, hoping to keep the topic on her life. "Where do you go from there?"

Rachel stabbed a piece of pasta and lifted a shoulder. "Right now I'm helping Alexis with the charity auction for the Pancreatic Cancer Research Foundation."

Impressed, Matt nodded in silent admiration.

"What's the auction? Do you have donations from area businesses?"

Rachel dropped her fork, pulled the napkin from her lap and dabbed the corners of her mouth. "We're auctioning men."

Matt stilled. "Excuse me?"

Those bright, beautiful eyes locked on his across the table. There was that mischievous gleam he'd seen from her in the past. He wasn't sure he wanted to know more.

"We're having a bachelor auction. Care to be Bachelor Fifteen?"

Four

Way to go. Nothing like blurting out her thoughts without easing into the request. Granted she'd promised Alexis she'd ask Matt for the favor, but Rachel probably could've done a better lead in.

"Bachelor Fifteen."

The words slid slowly through his sultry, kissable lips as he set his fork down and continued to hold her gaze without so much as blinking. She really needed to not stare at his mouth, and she absolutely should not be imagining them on hers.

Rachel cringed. "So, we need another bachelor and we were wanting one that would be fairly popular, and you came to town, we're friends, you've got that new title and…"

He sat still as stone.

"I'm rambling," she muttered. "You don't want the hype or the press. I get it. Forget I asked."

Rachel focused on the potatoes on her plate. Carbs were always the answer, especially when she'd just verbally assaulted their friendship.

"Is that why you came?" he asked.

Rachel immediately met his gaze. "What? No. I wanted to see you. I wanted you to meet Ellie. Earlier I was working on the auction and Alexis and I started talking and your name came up."

Matt offered that cocky, familiar smirk. "Is that right?"

He was clearly intrigued by the idea of being the topic of conversation, but she wasn't about to feed that ego.

"But don't feel obligated to agree just because we're friends. In fact, forget I asked."

Rachel started to reach for her sweet tea just as Ellie let out a cry of frustration. Pushing back in her chair, Rachel came to her feet, but Matt was quicker. He stood and crossed to the Pack 'n Play, reached down and lifted Ellie out.

Unable to look away, Rachel stared at the way Matt's large hands held on to her daughter. Ellie's little mouth slid into a frown as she stared at the stranger. She reached up and patted her tiny fingers against his mouth.

"Here, let me take her."

Matt shook his head as he made his way back to

the table. "She's fine. Enjoy your dinner and we can discuss this auction some more."

Rachel eased back into her seat as Matt sat back down in his own chair. Immediately Ellie's arm smacked Matt's glass over, spilling his drink into his plate of food.

"I'm so sorry." Rachel jumped up and grabbed her daughter before handing Matt her cloth napkin. "Let me go inside and get a towel. Go finish my plate and I'll get this cleaned up—"

Matt grabbed her arm. "Relax. Nobody's hurt here and it's just a spill. Maybe we should go inside where Ellie can play on the floor and we can sit on the sofa and have dinner?"

Rachel wanted to gather her child and their things and leave to save further embarrassment, but she knew that would be rude after all the trouble he'd gone to. So against her better instincts, she nodded.

"I think she's getting hungry," she replied. "Let me feed her and then I'll help clean and carry things inside."

"Take care of her. I'll take care of everything else."

Rachel stared for a moment until she realized he was serious. She couldn't help but think back to Billy, who hadn't wanted kids, who'd been flat out angry over the pregnancy. Yet here was Matt offering to care for Ellie while Rachel did something as simple as eat her dinner.

She shouldn't compare the two men. Sure they were friends, but they'd always been opposite. Billy had been the adventurer, the wanderer, which had been the initial draw for Rachel.

Matt was just around for a good time. He was content in Dallas, happy with life and work. He was well-grounded and only got away to travel to Galloway Cove.

Who wouldn't be happy owning their own island? At this point in her life, Rachel just wanted to own her own home, not the house Billy had bought and not some place her in-laws wanted her to have. She wanted to do life her way.

Several moments later, Ellie had been fed. After cleaning her up, Rachel scooted the coffee table off to the far wall and left an open area for Ellie to play in without hitting her head on the furniture.

Matt came back in and quickly had their food all set up, acting as if an infant hadn't just turned his steak and potatoes into tea soup.

"I'm really sorry about that," Rachel offered as he sat on the sofa next to her.

"Why do you keep apologizing? Just because I don't have children doesn't mean I'm going to get angry over an accident."

Rachel glanced down to Ellie who was quite content plucking the nose on the stuffed toy monkey. "I just never know how people will respond. Some people don't like children."

"I've never really seen myself in the role of a father, but I like kids. I mean, I highly doubt she knocked my glass down on purpose."

Rachel settled her plate into her lap. "You can eat at the table, you know. You don't have to sit here with me."

All of this was too familial, and being in a situation like this with Matt only made her fantasize about things she could never have…at least not with this man.

"Tell me more about the auction," he said, ignoring her previous statement.

"Matt, really—"

"Tell me."

His gruff command had her pulling in a deep breath. "Alright. The bachelor auction is going to raise funds for the Pancreatic Cancer Research Foundation. Alexis's grandmother and Gus's wife passed away from that. When Alexis invited me to come visit, I offered to help with the auction. I'm not quite finished with my marketing degree, but I'm thrilled to be doing something along the lines of where I want to be. Not only am I helping the cause—this will look great on a resume when I finish my degree."

"They're lucky to have you working on this," Matt stated with such conviction she turned to him in surprise .

"You have a lot of confidence for someone who hasn't seen me in a year."

Matt finished chewing before he replied. "I know you, Rachel. Maybe better than you know yourself. You're determined, headstrong and always looking out for everyone but yourself."

His blue eyes locked with hers, causing a warm melting sensation to spread through her.

"Alexis couldn't have chosen a better person for the job. You don't need a degree to have compassion."

She wasn't even sure how to respond to such praise. She hadn't been looking for a compliment. They finished their dinner in silence and Ellie played without interruption.

"Let me take the plates to the kitchen," Rachel said, reaching for Matt's empty dish.

"I've got it."

"You've done enough. I can take care of this."

His suite at The Bellamy was absolutely dreamlike. Rachel couldn't imagine being a guest here. She'd never want to leave.

"I invited you."

Matt took the dishes and headed toward the open kitchen area. Having a sexy man do domestic chores was something no woman could look away from. Added to that, the thin navy sweater he wore stretched beautifully across his broad shoulders, captivating her attention.

"You're not doing anything except telling me more about the auction," he stated. "What do I have to do as Bachelor Fifteen?"

Rachel laughed, more out of shock than humor. "You don't have to put yourself up for auction. We have guys who will bring in the goal Alexis is hoping to raise."

To Rachel's surprise, Matt didn't sit back on the sofa with her, but on the floor with Ellie. With one hand propped behind him, he rested his other arm on the knee he'd drawn up.

"So when a woman wins her dream guy onstage, or however you're doing it—"

"In the gazebo at the TCC clubhouse," she interjected.

He nodded. "Fine. So when a lady's knight in shining armor steps from the gazebo and they gaze into each other's eyes, then what?"

Rachel eased down to the floor as well and couldn't help but laugh. "It's probably not going to be that dramatic. But, the ladies are bidding on a fantasy date. Whatever that might be. One of our bachelors is a pilot, so the winner could also choose to be flown in his private jet to a nice dinner. All of the guys bring something different to the table, which is exactly what we want so we can appeal to a variety of women."

"And their checkbooks."

Rachel smiled and nodded. "Exactly."

"How many bachelors have an island?"

"None."

"Then count me in."

Rachel jerked back. Ellie crawled to her and climbed onto her lap. "Just like that you're offering yourself up?"

"It's one date, Rachel. I'm not marrying anyone. If it's for a good cause, and it is, I'm willing." He handed Ellie her monkey when she wobbled closer to him. "I'll match the donation of the bid made on me, as well."

She couldn't believe how easy this was. "You could just write a check if you're only wanting to help financially."

"Sounds like you don't want me to be on the auction block," he threw back with a quirked brow.

That's precisely what she sounded like because that's exactly how she felt. But she had no right, and she truly had no motive to keep him all to herself. Matt didn't belong to anyone, especially not his best friend's lonely widow.

"I just want you to be fully aware of what you're getting into."

His eyes held hers and they did that thing again, that thing where he seemed as if he could look right into her soul and grab onto her deepest thoughts. However, it was best for them both that he couldn't see her true feelings.

"I think I can handle myself," he murmured. "Will you be bidding?"

Rachel's heart thudded in her chest. She honestly hadn't given it much thought until the idea of Matt being up for grabs came to light. Could she actually bid on him? What would he think? Would he think she was trying to date him? That she wanted to start something beyond friendship? Or would he think she was saving him from the other women waving their paddles?

"Do you want me to bid on you?"

Why did her voice come out so husky like some sultry vixen? Because she certainly was no seductress. For pity's sake, her child had fallen asleep on her lap and Rachel was acting like some love-struck teen.

Matt lifted a shoulder. "What would your dream date be? We might be able to work out a deal and both get what we want."

What did that mean? Did he want a date with her?

Why the hell was this all so confusing now? When she'd been married to Billy and they'd all gone out with friends and had a good time, she and Matt would joke and laugh and there was never this crackling tension.

Crackling tension. What a great way to say sexual energy, though she had no idea if this was all one-sided or not. Or had this been there before and she'd never noticed? Surely she would've sensed it if Matt had been interested.

"I don't know what my dream date would be," she admitted. "I've never thought about it."

Matt reached over and Rachel thought for sure he was reaching for her, but he slid a wisp of a curl from Ellie's forehead. Rachel's heart flipped. She had no idea what to expect with Matt and his reaction to Ellie, but he'd put her needs ahead of anything else. The baby items on the patio had to have cost a ridiculous amount, and now he sat here acting so caring and doting toward her little girl as if this were the most natural thing in the world.

He settled his hand on her knee and Rachel realized he'd slid even closer. "What about a day out on my boat? You could relax and do nothing but get a suntan and snap your finger for another fruity drink."

Rachel tipped her head and smiled. "Do you honestly think I could relax and do nothing? When have you ever known me to laze around?"

Right now, though, it was getting rather difficult to think of anything because all she could concentrate on was his large, firm hand on her knee. Forget the fact a good portion of her lap had gone numb from Ellie's weight; she could most definitely feel Matt's searing touch.

"Okay, then, maybe a trip to Galloway Cove. You could swim, have dinner on the beach, get a massage from one of my staff."

Rachel shook her head. "I'm pretty sure I won't be bidding. First of all, I'm not sure I could afford you once the ladies see your credentials. And second, I couldn't leave Ellie for an entire day."

"If you bid on me and win, Ellie could come, too. I have on-site staff at every single one of my homes."

Of course he did. Billy had come from money, but that was nothing compared to the lifestyle Matt lived. Billy partied with his money, but Matt invested. He had homes, jets, an island and who knew how many cars. Most likely he had businesses on the side from the company he ran. Men like him never had just one business going because that wouldn't be smart. And Matt was one of the most intelligent people Rachel had ever known.

"I think I better just write a check to the foundation and stay behind the scenes."

Matt's thumb stroked over her knee. Back and forth, back and forth. The warmth through the fabric of her capris ironically sent shivers through her.

"Matt," she whispered, not knowing what to say but realizing this moment was getting away from them.

"What if I want you to bid on me?" he asked, never looking away from her. "Maybe I want to give you that day you need. Perhaps it's time someone makes you take time for yourself."

Rachel didn't know what to say. She'd seen Matt charm women in the past, but she'd never been on the receiving end. He was dead serious that he wanted her to bid on him. But if she did that, if they went off on some fantasy date, Rachel couldn't guarantee that she'd be able to avoid temptation. Matt had always held a special place in her heart, but she was seeing him in a whole different light now. Getting mixed up with him on a physical level would only end in heartache...and she had plenty of that to last a lifetime.

"You don't have to answer now," he added. He hadn't eased back, nor had he removed his hand. "But I'm all in under one condition."

She was almost afraid to ask.

"And that is?"

That cocky, signature Matt Galloway grin spread across his face. "You're the only one I'm dealing with. As in the photos that need taking and anything else that is needed from me for the auction itself. You're it for me."

That last sentence seemed to spear straight through that tough exterior she'd shielded herself with. Matt had that power, a power she'd always known he possessed, but she'd never fully realized the impact he could have on her until now.

"I'm not exactly a professional photographer," she reminded him.

"I recall your hobby behind the lens and I would bet anything you've kept up with it, especially to take pictures of Ellie." He slid his hand away, but eased forward until their faces were only a few inches apart. "Do we have a deal?"

Rachel simply nodded, unable to speak with him so close. She wasn't sure what she was getting herself into, but Alexis would be thrilled to have Matt as the headliner. Wasn't that the goal?

Five

Gus closed the tack box and blew out a sigh. He'd worked hard today, but he wouldn't have it any other way. Lone Wolf Ranch gave him the reason to get out of bed each day, especially since his beloved Sarah had passed. That made two women in his lifetime who had left an imprint on his heart. There was only so much heartache a man could take, and Gus had met his quota.

From here on out, he planned on devoting his every single day to his livestock, his ranch and his granddaughter. There was no way in hell his sweet Alexis could hook up with Daniel Clayton. That boy was nothing but trouble and the grandson of Rose Clayton…Gus's first love.

The Claytons were dead to him. He'd rather give

up his ranch than see their families merge…and he sure as hell wasn't giving up his ranch.

The years he and Rose spent together all seemed like a lifetime ago. In fact, it was. They'd been in love and Gus had worked his ass off to make sure he was ready for marriage before he set out to get approval from Rose's father.

Gus had never been so nervous, so excited, so ready to spend his life with the woman of his dreams. But when he'd come back, he'd discovered his beloved Rose had been married the year before to a man handpicked by her father.

Gus wasn't going down that road in his mind again. He'd traveled that path too many times to count, too many times wondering what the hell had happened. But in the end, he'd married Rose's best friend, Sarah, and they'd had a beautiful life together until she passed.

The rap of knuckles on wood had him turning from the stalls. Outlined in the doorway of his barn with the sun setting against her back stood Rose Clayton. He might as well have conjured her up from his thoughts. Lately his mind had been focused on her more than it should, but that was only because they were conspiring with each other…not that they were reconnecting. That love story had ended long ago.

"I hope this isn't a bad time," Rose stated, stepping into the barn.

She always appeared as if she were going to a tea

party at the country club, but as she strode through the barn filled with the smell of hay and horses, Gus got a lump in his throat. She looked absolutely beautiful here. Her pale pink capris and matching jacket with a crisp white shirt and gold necklace created quite the contrast to his filthy work clothes. She'd always been that way, though…a vast juxtaposition from him.

Damn it. He needed to focus on the present, and not waste his time dwelling on nostalgic memories.

"I'm just finishing up for the day," he replied, adjusting the tip of his Stetson. "You're lucky Alexis isn't around or she'd wonder what you were doing here."

"I actually just saw her getting out of her car in town so I knew it was a safe time."

The way she looked at him as she moved through the open space, the way she spoke so softly, all of it was so Rose. Everything about her was precise, well-mannered, captivating.

And he'd always been the man who wasn't good enough for her. Being pushed from her life was the last time he'd ever allowed anyone to make him feel inferior.

But he could look and even admit that she was more stunning now than she'd been forty years ago.

"I was wondering how the auction is shaping up," Rose stated, clutching her purse with both hands. "I hadn't heard from you in a few days and I didn't know what Alexis has said."

Why did Rose seem so nervous? She typically had

confidence he admired, even though they weren't friends—more like sworn enemies.

"Alexis and her friend Rachel were going over the list of names the other day. Daniel still hasn't fully committed even though he did allow us to put him on the roster. He told Rachel he was still on the fence, so you'll have to nudge him." He released a breath. "Rachel is doing the marketing and has all of his information and the headshot that you sent anonymously, but we'll need him to actually sign the contract."

Rose sighed. "That's what I was afraid of. I've told him he's a perfect bachelor. What woman wouldn't want to go out with a successful rancher? He has his own jet—he could take his fantasy date anywhere."

"But his fantasy date is my granddaughter," Gus reminded her tersely.

Rose pursed her pale pink lips and nodded. "I'll talk to him tomorrow."

"Alexis didn't seem all that pleased to see his name on the list when Rachel was going over it the other day."

"He'll be on that stage," Rose assured him. "We just have to make sure Alexis isn't the one bidding on him."

Gus smiled. "Oh, I'll have her busy when it's his turn. If I have to make up some backstage disaster, Alexis will not bid on Daniel. I've mentioned a few bachelors to her, but I'm pushing her toward Matt Galloway, Rachel's friend from Dallas. He seems perfect for my Lex."

Rose stared at him another moment before giving a curt nod. When the silence settled heavy between them, Gus propped his hands on his hips and tipped his head.

"Something else on your mind?" he asked.

She opened her mouth, then shut it. After a moment, she finally said, "No. That's all. I just want to keep this communication open if we're going to make sure this goes off exactly as planned."

Gus didn't believe her one bit. She could've called or texted. Showing up here was rash and dangerous. They might have ended things decades ago, but he still knew when she was lying.

"Rose."

"Were you happy?"

The question came out of nowhere and left him speechless for a second. From the soft tone, the questioning gaze, he knew exactly what she referred to.

"Of course."

He never understood the term *sad smile* until now. The corners of Rose's mouth tipped up, but her low lids attempted to shield the pain in her eyes.

"That's all I ever wanted," she whispered.

Gus started to take a step forward, but Rose eased back and squared her shoulders. That fast she'd gathered herself together and whatever moment had just transpired had vanished.

"I'll keep you posted about Daniel."

When she turned to go, Gus couldn't stop himself. "You were happy with Ed, weren't you?"

Rose said nothing as she slowly turned and offered him that same less-than-convincing smile. Then she walked away. Not a word, not a nod of agreement. Nothing but sadness.

What the hell had just happened? What was this cryptic visit all about?

Any time he'd seen Rose and Ed over the years he'd always assumed they were a happily married couple. Sure Gus had been brokenhearted when he and Rose split, but he'd moved on and so had she. They'd turned into totally different people, created their own families and lives.

Gus never got over his bitterness toward how he was treated, how Rose so easily threw aside what they'd had. But marrying Sarah had been the right thing. He'd loved her with his whole heart and still mourned her loss.

And he'd be damned if Alexis and Daniel tried hooking up again. The last thing the Slades and the Claytons needed was to circle back together. He didn't want Rose in his life in any capacity. That might be harsh and rude, but the Claytons weren't exactly friends.

There was a nice young man out there for Alexis... Daniel Clayton just wasn't him.

"Where's Alexis?"

Rachel glanced around the garden area at TCC, but only saw Gus striding toward her. The wide hat on his head shadowed his face, but she could still catch that smile.

"She couldn't make it, so I told her I'd come help."

"Really?" Rachel asked, then shook her head. "Sorry, that was rude. I'm just surprised you'd want to discuss flowers, seating arrangements and how we'll be setting up the stage."

"This charity is dear to me," he told her as he wrapped an arm around her shoulder. "I'll do anything to help the cause."

After a quick pat on her back, Gus dropped his arm and spun in a slow circle. "Well, this place could use some maintenance."

Rachel had had those exact thoughts as she'd stepped outside. She and Alexis had planned on meeting here so they could figure out various parts of the auction. Rachel was hoping to get some photos to help use for the promotional side of things. Like maybe one of the empty area where the bachelors would be on display. She could use a simple photo like that and change out different catchy phrases for social media.

Unfortunately, Rachel wasn't so sure the gazebo was the best place to show off the hunky men.

"I don't even know where to start," Rachel murmured.

Gus pulled in a deep breath and adjusted his hat. "Well, first thing we're going to do is get a professional in here. You tell me what you want, and I mean every bloom and color, and I'll see that it happens."

Gus Slade wasn't joking. His matter-of-fact tone

left no room for argument and she certainly wasn't about to turn away the help.

"I think everything out here needs to be dug up," she stated, waving her hand over the overgrown, neglected landscaping. "The gazebo could use a fresh coat of paint, too. Keep it white, definitely, and add some nice fat pots at the entrance. Something classy, yet festive. Maybe whites and golds—or should we add some red in the mix? I love the idea of the clean look with white and gold. Oh, poinsettias. We would definitely need those, too."

Gus laughed. "Honey, you better write all that down. I'll make some calls and get a crew out here. We'll get this place fixed up in no time."

"Hopefully they can make it magical on short notice. We only have a few months to get everything ready, and I'll still need to get some pictures to advertise after the work is done."

She wanted to showcase the auction site and make a fairy tale–like poster to entice women and pique their interest before revealing the bachelors. She figured she would do one bachelor per day on their social media sites; that way each man got his proper attention.

Gus rocked back on his heels and pulled his cell from his pocket. "Money can make a whole host of things happen when and how you want it. I'll make a couple of calls right now. Hang tight."

Rachel walked around, making mental notes. She took some random pictures on her phone to use for reference later. In her mind, she could easily see the grand garden area filled with a perimeter of festive blossoms, with white chairs lining the middle. She wasn't sure if any woman would be able to sit once the excitement of bidding started, but there was also a good possibility of some ladies getting weak in the knees. Their bachelor lineup even had Rachel ready to wave a paddle.

"All set."

Rachel shifted her focus back to Gus. "You found someone to come already?"

"I left a message with Austin Bradshaw. He did some work for me a few years back and there's nobody else I'd trust to do this job. I know he's good and he'll make sure it's done in the time frame I want."

If Gus was that confident, and footing the bill, Rachel was definitely onboard. Alexis would be thrilled, too.

"I can't thank you enough." Rachel patted his arm, then adjusted her purse on her shoulder. "So, I'll go back to the ranch and draw up the list in detail. I took some photos so I can remember exactly what I want, and where. I'll get that to you this evening."

"Sounds good. I'm sure I'll hear back from Austin today." Gus narrowed his gaze and grinned. "Do you have your sights set on any bachelors? You've seen each one, so you have an edge on the competition. Daniel Clayton has his own ranch. You seem to love that lifestyle."

First of all, the auction was only bidding for a date.

Second, Rachel was pretty sure Alexis would have something to say if her best friend bid on Daniel.

And third...there was only one man from the entire group she'd want to bid on, and she was still torn over what to do on that. Matt had flat out asked her to bid on him. She wasn't sure what to make of his demand, but she certainly wanted to take as much as she was able to from her savings and do just that. If she already had her degree and a job, she'd be able to donate more, but she certainly could spare some to a worthy cause.

"Ah, so there is a man," Gus drawled out. "Well, he's a lucky guy. And who knows, maybe a date will turn into more."

Rachel laughed and shook her head. "You're a hopeless romantic, Gus. But I'm a widow and a single mother. I'm not ready to jump into the dating pool, let alone make another trip down the aisle."

The older gentleman opened his mouth to speak, but his cell chimed from his pocket. "Hold that thought," he said, pulling the phone out.

Yeah, she wasn't about to keep that topic open. She couldn't bring herself to fully think what would happen if she actually bid on Matt.

A shiver crept over her and she could chalk it up to nothing but pure desire. When she'd had dinner in his suite the other night, she was certain he would've closed the gap between them and kissed her. She'd seen the passion in his eyes and she hadn't missed the way his eyes dropped to her mouth and lingered.

Rachel wrapped her arms around her midsection and attempted to cool her heated thoughts. This kind of thinking was counterproductive, not to mention dangerous. She needed Matt to remain a friend, nothing more. She'd loved him like that for years. Yes, she was still hurt and she still deserved an explanation as to why he vanished, but this was Matt and she couldn't stay mad at him. She realized he'd been hurting, too, when Billy passed.

"That was Austin," Gus said. "He said he'll meet me out here tomorrow morning and look over your list. He'll start as soon as he gets all the supplies in."

"Wow," Rachel exclaimed. "That was fast."

Gus shrugged. "He's pushing a few jobs back for this. I just need to clear everything with the TCC board, but that won't be an issue."

Gus Slade was one powerful man who got what he wanted, when he wanted it. He reminded her of another strong man.

Rachel sighed. Did every thought lately circle back to Matt? Because every time her mind headed toward him, she got that tingling sensation all over again. Hard as she tried, there was no controlling her imagination or this new ache that seemed to accompany each thought of him.

"I truly appreciate this," she told him. "Alexis will be so thrilled."

"You're doing so much more than just marketing," Gus added. "We need to be thanking you."

"Just give me a good reference when I get my degree and need a job."

"Consider it done."

Gus wrapped his arm around her shoulder and started walking back toward the entrance to the clubhouse. "What do you say we grab some lunch? My treat."

"I really should get back to Ellie."

Ellie had been left with a member of Gus's staff. Each person at Lone Wolf Ranch absolutely doted over Rachel's daughter, so there was no doubt she was in good hands.

"Another hour won't matter," Gus stated. "Call and check on her if it makes you feel better."

Rachel nodded. "You're spoiling me and I might never leave."

As he led her toward the restaurant inside TCC, Gus laughed. "You have an open invitation to stay at Lone Wolf as long as you like."

Her in-laws probably wouldn't like that idea, but the longer Rachel stayed in Royal, the more she felt like she'd finally come home.

Six

Matt glanced at the Halloween-costume party invitation that had been hand delivered to his suite. The board at TCC was hosting the festive event and apparently the entire town was invited.

What the hell would he do at a costume party? Was there a man in his right mind who actually wanted to dress up?

Granted he could always go as a disgruntled CEO or aimless wanderer since he had no clue what the hell he wanted in his life right now. Something was missing, something that his padded bank account couldn't buy. Being back in Royal stirred something in him he hadn't felt in a long, long time. There was a sense of community here and people always looking out for each other…something he didn't see in Dallas.

Tossing the invitation on the counter, Matt grabbed his keys and headed to the elevator just off his living area. He planned to do a drive-by of his grandfather's place today to see exactly what he was dealing with, and then he had to pick up Rachel so she could take some pictures of him for the auction.

Whatever possessed him to agree to such madness? Auctioning himself off sounded absurd, and he preferred to choose his own dates, thank you very much. It wasn't like he had trouble finding female companions. So how did he end up here?

Oh, that's right. Rachel had asked. Things were as simple and as complicated as that. He couldn't say no to her, no matter what she wanted. Rachel was… well, she was special and she deserved better than the thoughts and fantasies he'd been harboring for years.

More times than he cared to admit he'd imagined her in his bed, all of them from the island mansion to his Dallas home. He'd pictured her swimming in the ocean wearing nothing but his touch and a sated smile.

Matt attempted to shove thoughts of Rachel from his mind as he drove toward his grandfather's old farm. The place had sat empty for years. After Matt's parents had passed, the land had been willed to him. He had been too busy in Dallas to deal with it, but now, well, he could sure as hell use the outlet.

He and his partner weren't seeing eye to eye, and

that was partially due to Matt not being happy in the place he was at in his life. Every day he went to work, and no matter how successful he was, there always seemed to be a void.

Maybe finding a contractor and pushing through some renovations would help. It certainly couldn't hurt.

Matt pulled into the drive overgrown with grass and weeds. The white two-story farmhouse sat back, nestled against the woods. The old barn off to the right actually looked to be in better shape than the house itself.

Swallowing the lump of emotion, Matt stared at the front porch that looked like a good gust of Texas wind could knock it down. He recalled spending his summers with his grandfather, learning all about farm life, about hard work and seeing it pay off. Matt owed everything to that man. Without Patrick Galloway, Matt wouldn't be the successful oil tycoon he was today.

As a young boy, he hadn't realized all the life lessons being instilled, but now looking back, there was no doubt he was being shaped.

Matt smiled as he continued to look at the porch. The creaky swing that hung on one end was gone, but he could easily see it in his mind. His grandfather would sit there and play the harmonica while Matt sat on the top step with two sticks and played faux drums.

Damn it. He missed the simpler times. He missed

his parents, his grandfather, those carefree summer nights followed by sweat-your-ass-off workdays.

He'd call a contractor tomorrow. This wasn't something he was going to leave to his assistant, though she was fabulous. Matt planned on handling every bit of this personal project himself.

His cell rang through the speakers of his truck, but he ignored the call when his partner's number flashed on the screen. Matt would call him back later. Right now he wanted to get to Rachel and get this photo shoot over with. She'd requested he wear a suit so she could capture him in his element. Although it was true that business attire was part of his daily life, he'd like to be a bit more casual for this shoot.

Then again, this wasn't his charity and he wasn't the one bidding. Good grief. He was honestly going to stand on a stage and watch women waving paddles around just to go on a date with him.

There was only one woman he wanted to win that bid. He'd have to do some convincing, though. Rachel had seemed a little hesitant and he couldn't blame her. He'd up and deserted her after Billy's funeral, then he'd dropped back into her life unexpectedly, and followed that by making it clear he wouldn't mind kissing her.

Yeah, he saw her lids widen and heard her breath hitch when he inched closer as they sat on the floor of his suite. Had Ellie not been between them, Matt would have pulled Rachel to him and taken a sample of something he'd coveted for far too long. Just one taste. At least that's what he told himself he needed to get over the craving.

Matt pulled out of the drive and headed toward Lone Wolf Ranch. Ten minutes later, he was turning into the sprawling estate with a wrought iron arch over the entrance. This was Royal, small town charm mixed with money, lots of it, and a big-city feel. Matt could easily see the pull to live here, and he was banking on that for when he renovated his grandfather's farm. The real estate market was booming and he knew he'd have no trouble selling.

The thought didn't settle well with him, but he didn't need the place. He had his ten-thousand-square-foot home in Dallas and his own island, for pity's sake. He traveled when and where he wanted. He couldn't hold on to the old farmstead simply for nostalgia.

As he approached the massive main house, Rachel came bounding down the stairs. She smiled and waved. There was no denying the punch of lust to the gut. She wore another one of those long, curve-hugging dresses that she probably thought was comfortable, but all he could think was how fast he could have that material shoved up to her waist and joining their bodies after years of aching to have no barriers between them.

There wasn't a doubt in Matt's mind that the real thing would put the fantasy to shame.

Damn. He seriously needed to get a grip.

Rachel opened the truck door, and had he not

been imagining her naked he would've gotten out and opened her door for her.

"Hey." She hopped in and set the camera bag between them. "Are you ready for this?"

A day alone with Rachel? Hell yeah.

"I guess so." He turned toward her slightly. "This suit okay?"

He absolutely relished the way her eyes raked over him. Sure his ego was larger than most, but the only woman he wanted was looking at him as if she wanted him right back.

"It will do."

Leave it to Rachel to knock him down a peg. With a low chuckle, Matt put the truck in gear and headed back down the drive.

"So, where are we going?" she asked.

He'd insisted on the location of the shoot as well as her being the photographer. If he'd told her ahead of time where he was taking her, she would've balked at the suggestion.

"I'll keep it a surprise for now."

Rachel clicked her seatbelt into place and settled back in the seat. "As long as I'm back in time to give Ellie a bath. I was actually ordered by Alexis to go have fun. She thinks we're dating."

Interesting. "What have you been saying about me to your host family?"

Rachel laughed, the sultry sound flooding the small space. "Gus is a romantic at heart and Alexis, well, she's just excited I'm talking to any man."

Matt gripped the steering wheel. "Surely you've been on a date in the last year."

"Why would you think that?"

He pointed the truck toward the edge of town, heading for the airstrip. "Because you're a beautiful, passionate woman, Rachel."

"I'm a widow and a single mother."

Gritting his teeth, Matt weighed his words carefully. "So you've reminded me before, but that doesn't mean you don't get to have a social life. Do you plan on staying single until Ellie moves out of the house?"

Rachel blew out a sigh and turned to face the side window. "I don't want to argue with you, Matt. It's not like I can just pick up and date anyone I want. I have a child to think about now and she has to come first. We're a package deal, so I can't just bring men in and out of her life."

He didn't say another word, because he also didn't want to argue, but there were plenty of thoughts circling around in his mind. Maybe he didn't want a ready-made family and marriage and picket fences, but he wanted Rachel. He wanted to prove to her that she was still alive, that just because her life had changed dramatically didn't mean she had to give up her wants and needs.

Maybe this bachelor auction was exactly what he needed to make his case. If he was going to put himself on display like a piece of meat, he was sure as hell going to use it to his advantage. Rachel was about to come to grips with the fact that she could still be a mother *and* a woman. A passionate, desirable woman.

"What are we doing here?"

Rachel stared at the small airstrip and the private plane with a man dressed all in black waiting at the base of the stairs. For the past ten minutes, she and Matt had ridden in silence. He simply didn't understand where she was coming from in regard to her dating life and she wasn't going to keep explaining her situation.

"You wanted pictures, right?" He pulled the truck to a stop and killed the engine. "We're going to Galloway Cove."

She jerked in her seat and faced him. "What? But, you're in a suit and I thought we were doing office-type images since you're a CEO."

Matt shrugged. "You want me in the auction, I'm calling the shots on how I'm portrayed. Don't worry, there's an office in my beach house."

He hopped out of the truck without another word and circled the hood. When he opened her door, Rachel still couldn't believe he was taking her to his island for the photo shoot. She couldn't be alone with him on a secluded island. That screamed *cliché* with all of these newly awakened emotions she had toward him. Was he purposely trying to get her alone?

Anticipation and nerves swirled together deep in her gut. Was he trying to seduce her?

"Why don't we just take some of you standing in front of your plane?" she suggested, trying not to sound as flustered as she felt. "That would fuel any woman's fantasy for the auction."

Because this suit was totally doing it for her.

Matt's striking blue eyes held her captivated as he leaned closer. "Maybe there's only one woman I want to fantasize about me."

Even with the truck door open, there still didn't seem to be enough air to fill her lungs. This was Matt, her friend. Her very sexy, very dynamic friend whose broad shoulders filled out his suit to the point it should be illegal for him to walk around in public.

The stirrings of desire hit her hard. Harder than when she'd wanted him to kiss her in his penthouse suite. Why now? Why did he drop back into her life and make her question the direction she was moving? She didn't have time for desire or kisses or hot, sultry looks from a man who used to be her rock. She wasn't looking for anything akin to lust or attraction right now. Like she had the time to worry about another relationship.

His dark blue eyes slid from her eyes to her lips.

"Don't do that," she scolded.

His mouth kicked up in a cocky smirk. "What's that?"

"Try to be cute or pretend like you want to kiss me."

Matt laughed. "Leave it to you to not skirt around the situation. I'm not pretending, Rachel. I plan on kissing you. You won't know when, but that's your warning."

Well, hell. Apparently the gauntlet she just threw down had awakened the beast. The real question was, how long had he been lying in wait?

Matt leaned across the seat, his solid chest brushing hers, his lips coming within a breath. Rachel inhaled, the subtle movement causing her sensitive breasts to press further against his hard body. She hadn't been aroused like this in so long, she couldn't trust her judgment right now. Her mind was all muddled and her hormones were overriding common sense. But she had to remain in control…at all costs.

"Relax," he murmured.

The click of her belt echoed in the cab of the truck and Matt eased away, taking her hands in his to help her out. He reached back in for the camera bag and flung it over his big, broad shoulder before closing the door.

Finally, she could breathe. Even though he was holding her hand as they walked across the tarmac, Rachel could handle that.

What she could not handle, however, was that promise or threat or whatever he'd issued when he'd warned her of the kiss. The way he'd looked at her, rubbed against her and put naughty, *R*-rated thoughts inside her head.

They shouldn't be kissing. What they needed to do was get photos and focus on the auction…an auction where other women would be writing big fat checks to score a date with this handsome, prominent bachelor. He wasn't hers…not in that way.

"I'm not going to bid on you," she stated, as if that was her mega comeback for the way he'd got her all hot and bothered in the truck, and then strolled along as if nothing had changed between them. "You need to get that through your thick head."

"Of course you will."

Rachel jerked her hand from his and marched onward toward the steps of the plane. Arrogant bastard. Why was she friends with him again?

The pilot smiled and nodded as he welcomed her on board. Rachel climbed the stairs and was stunned at the beauty and spaciousness of the plane. She'd known Matt had his own aircraft, but she'd never been inside it. She'd never been to Galloway Cove, either. When they all hung out, Billy, Matt and her, Matt usually came to her house or they all met at their favorite pub in Dallas.

But Rachel wasn't going to stroke his ego anymore and comment on the beauty of the details or even act like she was impressed.

She went to the dark leather sofa that stretched beneath the oval windows, took a seat on one end and then fastened her safety belt. Matt and the pilot spoke but she couldn't make out their words. Didn't matter. She knew where they were going, knew Matt's intentions, but that didn't mean she would give in. He still owed her answers, and being on a plane with nowhere for him to run was exactly where she planned on getting them.

Rachel shifted and kept looking out the window as Matt came back and took a seat—of course on the same sofa, but at least on the opposite end. It took all of her willpower not to just bombard him with all the questions she'd been dying to ask since he'd disappeared from her life. But she would. She wanted him to get nice and comfortable with his situation first. He thought he was calling the shots, but she was about to flip their positions.

Seven

Rachel had been quiet during takeoff. Too quiet. Her gaze never wavered from the window. The flight took about an hour and a half from Royal and Matt had to admit, he was worried.

She was plotting something. She was pissed, if the thin lips and the sound of her gritting teeth was any indicator. Perhaps he'd been too forward earlier, but damn it, he'd held out for years and he was done skirting around his attraction. She deserved to know how much he wanted her. He couldn't go at this any slower. At this rate they'd be in a nursing home before he got to first base.

He might want nothing more than to see where this fierce physical attraction went, but perhaps she was on the same page. He knew she was more of a happily-ever-after girl, but perhaps she wanted to just have a good time and not think about commitments for a while.

That was plausible…right? Or was he just trying to justify his actions to himself so he didn't feel like an ass for making a move on his late friend's wife?

"Why don't you just say what you're stewing about and let's move on?" He couldn't stand the damn silence another second.

She didn't move one bit, except her eyes, which darted to him. Oh, yeah. She was pissed.

"Fine. Start with Billy's funeral and your immediate absence after."

Hell. He'd known this was coming—he'd rehearsed the speech in his head over and over. However, nothing prepared him to actually say the words aloud.

"I know you were hurting—"

"Hurting? You *crushed* me," she scolded. "Billy's death tore me apart and I needed you. I was pregnant, scared, facing in-laws who were smothering me, and I just wanted my friend."

He'd crushed her. That was a bitter pill to swallow and he had no excuse other than he was selfish and trying to do what he thought was best at the time. But she'd needed him, and he worried more that he'd take them into unknown territory while she was still vulnerable. He'd been a total prick, but hindsight was a bitch.

"I texted." That was lame even to his own ears. "I just… I needed space."

She turned her attention back to the window. "An entire year," she murmured. Then she shifted in her seat to fully face him, anger and pain flooding her eyes with unshed tears, and she might as well have stabbed him and twisted the knife.

"Would you have contacted me had we not run into each other? Or were you only friends with me because of Billy?"

"No." She had to know that above all else. "What you and I shared had nothing to do with Billy."

And everything to do with him.

"I would've reached out to you, Rachel," he said softly. "I missed you."

"Well, that's something," she whispered, almost in relief.

Matt immediately unbuckled his belt and slid closer, taking her hands even though she tried to pull back. "Look at me, damn it. Did you honestly believe that because he died I was just done with you? With us?"

"What else was I supposed to think? I mean, we were close for so long and then I didn't see you. I went by your house and your housekeeper told me you were on vacation. You answered my texts in short sentences as if I was bothering you. Then... nothing."

Yeah, because he'd hidden away at his home on Galloway Cove until he could go back to Dallas and not risk telling Rachel how he'd felt for years. There were things about Billy she didn't know, and it had taken all of his strength to keep those secrets to himself. But those last few days of his life, Billy hadn't only argued with Rachel. He and Matt had finally had it out and Matt had issued an ultimatum. Rachel didn't deserve to be treated like she wasn't the most important thing in Billy's world. Billy accused Matt of always wanting her, and fists started flying.

"Matt?"

He blinked away from the memories and squeezed her hands. He couldn't tell her about all of that. He sure as hell wasn't going to tell her when Billy died, because she was suffering enough. What would the point be in telling her now that her husband had been unfaithful? There was no reason at all to drudge up the past and make her feel even worse.

"I had to get away," he croaked out, cursing himself for showing weakness. He swallowed the lump of guilt and the ache that accompanied his desire for her. "I knew Billy's parents and brother would watch out for you. I needed some time to myself."

"I still don't understand why so long." She stared back at him, studying his face as if truly trying to understand his way of thinking. "I missed you."

There was only so much a man could take, and those last three words sliced through his last thread of control.

Matt gripped her face between his hands and covered her mouth with his. For a half second he had a sliver of fear that she would push him away. She didn't pull back, but she stiffened, hopefully from shock and not from repulsion.

Yes. That's all he could think as he slid his tongue through the seam of her lips. He'd been right. The real thing didn't even compare to his fantasies. Not only that, no other woman had ever made him so damn achy and needy like Rachel.

The second she relaxed, Matt shifted his body to cover hers as she leaned against the back of the sofa. Her hands came up to his shoulders, her fingertips curling around him as if to hold him in place. Like he was going anywhere after finally getting her in this position. If only he could shut out the rest of the world and stay like this with her until he'd finally exorcised her out of his system.

Matt wanted to rip her dress off, discard this ridiculous suit and lay her flat out, taking everything he'd craved for damn near ten years.

But he couldn't. He respected Rachel, and a kiss was one thing, but taking it to the next level was another. And if that was the route they were going to go, he wasn't dragging her. No, if she wanted him, she'd have to show him.

At least now she knew where he stood.

Matt pulled back, still keeping her face between his palms. He rested his forehead against hers and fell into the same breathing pattern as her.

"Well, you did warn me."

He laughed. He couldn't help it. "I won't apologize."

Rachel tipped her head back. Heavy lids half covered her expressive eyes, and her lips were plump and wet from his passion. She stared at him for a moment before she seemed to close in on herself, blinking and pulling in a deep breath.

"I didn't ask for an apology," she stated. "We kissed. It's over. We're friends, so this shouldn't be a big deal."

Processing her words, Matt slowly released her and sat back. *Shouldn't be a big deal?* He'd waited to touch her, to taste her for a damn long time, and she just brushed it aside as no big deal? It sure as hell was a huge deal, and she knew it.

"I told you before you're a terrible liar."

Rachel's eyes widened a fraction before she eased away from him and came to her feet. Considering there was nowhere for her to escape, he sat and watched as she paced. She not only paced—she held her fingertips to her lips. The egotistical side of him liked to think she was replaying their kiss—he sure as hell was.

"Let me get this straight." She paced toward the kitchen, then back toward him. "We've been friends since college. I marry your best friend. He passes away. I don't hear from you for too damn long, and now you want to…what? What is it you want from me?"

Everything.

No. That wasn't true. He didn't want marriage or children. He'd never considered any of that part of his life plan. Billy hadn't, either, but when he'd married Rachel, he'd been in love. It was the whole family thing that had put him off-kilter.

"Maybe I want to prove to you that you're ready to get back out in the world and date." The thought of her with another man prickled the hairs on the back of his neck and made him fist his hands in his lap. "You returned that kiss, Rachel. Don't tell me you don't have needs."

She snapped her attention back to him, crossing her arms over her chest. "My needs are none of your concern."

They were every bit his concern.

"Sit down," he demanded. "You're making me dizzy watching you pace back and forth."

She narrowed her eyes before turning and taking a seat in one of the two swivel-style club chairs on the opposite side. She crossed her legs and adjusted her dress over her knees, but that did nothing to squelch his desire.

Matt still tasted her on his lips. He still felt her grip on his shoulders. What would she be like when she fully let her guard down and let him pleasure her? Because that moment would happen. Right now she had to get used to the kiss—there would be more—and then he'd slowly reawaken the passion he knew was buried deep inside.

Matt's single-story beach home with its white exterior and white columns along the porch might have been the most beautiful thing Rachel had ever seen.

The lush greenery looked like a painting, and the various pieces of driftwood in the landscaping were the perfect added touch.

Rachel could easily see why he kept this island a secret. Some men would've thrown parties here at the opulent beachfront home, but Matt kept his life more private.

And that privacy was one of the main differences between him and Billy. Her late husband liked to live large, celebrate life every single day by going on adventures or partying.

It was difficult not to compare the two friends, especially now that she'd kissed Matt. No. Correction. He'd kissed her. And boy did he ever kiss. That man's mouth was potent enough she was still tingling. What the hell would happen to her if he actually got his hands on her?

The idea had hit her the moment he'd touched his mouth to hers and part of her had wanted him to take things further.

Which was why she'd had to sit on the other side of the plane for the duration of the flight. Her mind was clouded, that's all. She didn't want her best friend…did she?

Being on the other side of the plane hadn't stopped Matt from staring at her, looking like the Big Bad Wolf deliciously wrapped in an Italian suit. Predators apparently came in all forms and hers was billionaire oil tycoon posing as her friend. Because the way he'd stared made her feel like he could see right through her clothes to what lay underneath.

If he saw her saggy tummy and stretch marks, maybe he wouldn't be so eager. She wouldn't change her new mommy body for anything, though. Ellie was the greatest thing that had ever happened to her.

"Where do you want me?"

That low, sultry tone wrapped Rachel in complete arousal. Damn that man for making her want, making her think things she really shouldn't. She was human, after all, and she couldn't turn off her emotions or her needs. Surely there was some unwritten rule about lusting after your late husband's best friend.

Rachel turned from the wall of windows facing the stunning ocean view and met Matt's gaze from across the living room. He'd told her to look around and see which room would be best, and that had been nearly a half hour ago. She wasn't sure where he'd gone or what he was doing, but even her time alone in this stunning house hadn't cooled her off from that most scintillating plane ride.

"I thought you were calling the shots," she tossed back. "Granted the other guys I photographed didn't care where I put them."

Matt's eyes narrowed. "I thought you weren't comfortable taking my picture for this. You didn't say you'd done the others."

Rachel shrugged. "It saved money and I enjoy it. I never said I didn't want to take your picture, by the way. I simply said I wasn't a professional. You should've asked someone else."

One slow, calculated step at a time, Matt closed the distance between them. "And why is that, Rachel? Afraid of what you're feeling?"

She swallowed and tipped her chin. "I'm not afraid of anything. Now back off and stop trying to seduce me."

He reached out and smoothed her hair from her face before dropping his hand. "I'm not trying to seduce you. When I seduce you, you'll know it."

When.

The bold term had anticipation and arousal pulsing through her. This was getting them nowhere except dangerously close to the point of no return for their friendship.

"Are you willing to throw away our friendship for a quick romp?" she countered.

"Oh, honey. It won't be quick. I assure you." He stepped back and spread his arms wide. "Now, where do you want me?"

Why did he keep phrasing it like that?

Focus.

Rachel clutched the camera bag on her shoulder and nodded toward the hallway. "Let's start in your office. We'll do some professional shots and then I'll have you take off the jacket and tie, and roll up your sleeves and we'll do some casual ones outside. You've got such gorgeous landscaping and pool, it would be a shame not to grab some there."

"What about the waterfall?"

Rachel shook her head in amazement. "You have a waterfall? I seriously need to get my own island."

Matt laughed. "I'll show you when we're done. Maybe you'll want some shots there, as well."

A photo of this rich, gorgeous oil tycoon posing in front of a waterfall…yup, that would certainly have all the ladies drooling. Not her, of course, but the others who were bidding.

"You might just decide to bid on me yet," he drawled.

"Don't get too cocky."

"If I wasn't cocky, I wouldn't have gotten where I am today. And I prefer to use the term *confident*."

Rachel rolled her eyes and headed toward the other end of the house, where the office was. "And I prefer to leave our friendship intact, so keep those lips to yourself."

"Whatever you want," he murmured as she passed by. But his low, seductive tone indicated she'd want something else entirely, and damn it, he was right.

Eight

Rachel was going to need to take a dip in the pool to cool off. Mercy sakes. She'd thought Matt adorned in a three-piece suit, leaning against his desk with his arms crossed over his massive chest, flashing an arrogant smirk at the camera was sexy, but that was nothing compared to the images she currently snapped of him in the waterfall.

As in, *in* the waterfall. He'd rolled up his pant legs to his calves, folded his shirt sleeves onto those impressive forearms, and then untucked and unbuttoned the damn thing.

Oh, he was playing dirty and he knew it. It would serve him right if she let some wealthy socialite bid on him and then make him fulfill some fantasy date.

But would he kiss that faceless woman good-night? Would he pour every bit of his body and soul into that kiss like he had with her?

Jealousy didn't sit well with Rachel. She'd experienced it with her own husband in the final days of their marriage when she suspected infidelity, and she sure as hell didn't want to experience it again. Matt was a ladies' man, his newly appointed title made that crystal clear. No way would she ever want to get involved with a player again, and she wasn't sure if she'd ever be ready for another committed relationship.

"I think we have enough," she shouted over the cascading water.

Matt raked his wet hands through his hair, making the black strands glisten beneath the sun. In an attempt to ignore the curl of lust in her belly, Rachel scrolled through the images she'd taken over the last couple of hours.

The only problem she saw with each picture was that each one was absolute perfection, which said nothing of her photography skills and everything of the subject on the other side of the lens.

"Put your camera down."

Rachel glanced up. Matt still remained in the water, the bottom of his pants soaked, his shirt clinging like transparent silk against his tanned, muscular chest.

"What?"

"Get in the water. Work is over."

"Then we should head back."

She could *not* get into that water with him. Then her clothes would get clingy and he'd probably touch her or kiss her again, and at this point she wasn't sure she would be able to ignore the aching need. There wasn't a doubt in her mind Matt would set her world on fire; it was everything that came afterward that worried her.

She'd been without a man for so long…*too long*. She simply couldn't trust her erratic emotions right now.

Matt stalked toward her like some god emerging from the water. Droplets ran down his exposed skin and she was so riveted she couldn't look away. Part of her even imagined licking each and every one, and that only added fuel to the proverbial flames.

How had he put this spell on her and why was she letting him? Oh, right. Because she was on a slippery slope and barely hanging on.

When he reached for her hand, Rachel set her camera down on a rock. He urged her forward.

"I can't get wet," she protested, though her feet were following him. "I don't have extra clothes."

He walked backward, his eyes never wavering from hers. "Take off your dress and we won't have a problem."

"You're not getting me out of my clothes."

The smirk, that raised brow, the way he kept walking her toward the water's edge…damn it. He took her statement as a challenge.

"Matt, we can't do this."

Cool water slid over her toes, over her ankles, soaking the bottom of her dress. She was losing a battle she wasn't sure she ever had a fair fight in.

"No one is here to tell us not to."

"I'm telling us not to," she argued. "This isn't right."

"Says who? Tell me you're not attracted to me, Rachel. Tell me you didn't kiss me right back and you haven't been thinking of it every second since."

She chewed on her bottom lip to prevent a lie from slipping out…and also to hold the truth inside. But her silence was just as telling as if she'd admitted her true feelings.

"It's just water," he crooned. "Nothing to be afraid of."

"I told you before, I'm not afraid." She pulled her hand from his and lifted her dress, bunching it in her fist at her side. "Is this how you get all your women? You use that sultry voice, that heavy-lidded gaze and…" She waved up and down at his bare chest.

"All of my women?" he repeated. "Watch it, Rachel. I'll start to think you care about my sex life."

She'd never given it much thought before now. And in the past several hours, Matt and sex had consumed nearly all of her thoughts.

Without thinking, she pulled from his grasp and leaned down, scooped up some water and splashed him right in the face. He sputtered for a second before flicking the excess away. Rachel couldn't help but laugh at his shocked expression, but then that surprise turned to menace.

"You think that's funny, do you?"

In a lightning-flash movement, he scooped her up into his big, strong arms and headed toward the waterfall.

"No!" she squealed. "Don't drench me, Matt, please. I'm sorry! I'll do anything, just don't—"

Water covered her entire body, chilling her instantly. Rachel squeezed her eyes shut and held her breath as she wrapped her arms around Matt's neck and clung tight. She turned her face toward his neck, trying to shield herself from the pounding spray. A moment later, he shifted and the water was behind her.

Rachel blinked the water from her eyes and glanced up. Matt stared down at her with even more raw, elemental desire than she'd ever seen. Billy had never looked at her that way…no one had.

Easing her to her feet, Matt kept an arm banded around her waist and cupped the side of her face with his other hand. Rachel's heart pounded in her chest. She needed to stop this before things went any further, but she hadn't done a very good job at stopping the progress up to this point.

"I want you," he muttered against her mouth. His words were barely audible over the rushing waters.

"I know."

He tipped her back, leaning over her, still very much in control over her body…physically and emotionally. Those blue eyes locked on hers.

"Tell me no and we'll walk out of here and get

back on the plane. My pilot is there and ready when we are."

He'd just handed over total control to her and with one word she could end it all…or take what he'd presented to her wrapped in a delicious package.

And there was really no decision to be made here. Because, in the end, she wasn't going to deny herself. She had basic needs—there was nothing shameful about that. Besides, this was Matt. They were friends; he wasn't looking for more and neither was she.

One time. Just this once, be selfish.

Rachel gripped his face and pulled his mouth down to hers. In the next instant, Matt wrapped his arms around her waist, filling his hands with her rear. The warmth of his touch through the cool material warmed her instantly.

She slid her hands through his wet hair, clutching onto him as he continued to tip her backward. There was no way he'd let her fall, though. His grip was too tight, his mouth too powerful, his need practically radiating from him. She wasn't going anywhere.

His hips ground into hers and the thin layer of wet clothes might as well have been nonexistent. Except it was and proved to be a most frustrating barrier. She'd never felt this overwhelming need before, never had the feeling of all-consuming passion, like she couldn't control herself.

It had never been this way with Billy.

No. For right now she was going to be completely closed off from reality and anything that threatened to steal her happiness. Damn it, she was going to take what she wanted…what Matt wanted. How long had he desired her? Did seeing her again spark something inside him?

Oh, my. Had he wanted her before?

"You're thinking too hard," he rasped against her mouth.

His hands came to her shoulders and gripped the straps of her maxi dress. He yanked them down, the clingy material pulling the cups of her bra as well, instantly exposing her breasts.

She didn't have time to worry about her body or what he thought, because his mouth descended downward and Rachel arched against him as he drew one tight nipple into his mouth.

"Matt," she moaned.

"Say it again," he demanded. "I want my name on your lips."

She didn't think he'd heard her over the rushing water, but she definitely heard him. From the command, she had to guess that he was just as turned on as she was at this point.

Rachel yanked on the material of his shirt, but it clung to his biceps. He eased back just enough to remove the garment and toss it in the general direction of the shore.

Instantly her eyes went to the ink over his shoulder. She traced her finger over the eagle's wings that spanned around to the back.

"This is new."

When he trembled beneath her touch, she wondered just how much control she had here. More than she'd initially thought.

When her eyes darted to his face, she noted the clenched jaw, the heavy lids, the blue eyes that had darkened with arousal.

So much hit her all at once that it was like truly seeing Matt for the first time…and recognizing the secret yearnings he'd kept locked up inside for so long. "I never knew."

"Now you do."

Yeah, she did. And she'd have to worry about that later. Her body was humming and zinging and doing all of the other happy dances that accompanied the heady anticipation of having really great sex. But she'd never been this charged before, never wanted a man so bad. Knowing that he wanted her just as much…well, that only fueled her desire.

With more confidence than she'd ever had, Rachel pushed her dress all the way down until it puddled around her waist. She shimmied just enough to let it fall before she stepped out of it. With her bra barely covering her and her panties beneath the surface, she felt more exposed than ever.

Who the hell had sex outside in the middle of the day? The sun shone bright down on the pair, the water rushed beside them and a butterfly had literally just flown by. It was as if she'd already bid on her best friend and was living out the fantasy date she never knew she even wanted.

On a growl, Matt picked her up and headed toward the shoreline. Her legs instantly wrapped around his waist. This was seriously happening. If she deliberated too much about all the reasons this was a bad idea, she might back out, so she cleared her head of all rational thought.

Matt sat her down once again, this time her toes landing on the lush ground cover that ran along the edge of the waterfall. In seconds he'd discarded his clothes, and Rachel was too busy admiring the mouthwatering view to realize he'd gripped the edge of her panties. The material fell away as he gave a yank and they ripped clear off her body.

"Matt," she cried.

"I'm done waiting."

He enveloped her into his arms, gently taking her to the ground, but he rolled beneath her so that she was on top. Instantly her legs straddled his hips. Her hands went up, ready to cover her torso.

"No," he commanded as he took her hands away. "I want to see all of you. Don't be ashamed of something so beautiful."

Beautiful? Not how she'd describe her post-pregnancy body, but the way Matt's eyes caressed her skin had her almost believing him.

We don't have protection. The thought slid into her mind and she wondered if he'd stop. "I'm on birth control even though I haven't been with anyone since Billy, and even that was a couple months before his death."

The night Ellie had been conceived, actually. But that was a story she didn't want to plunk down right here between them.

"I've never been without protection, Rachel. I know I'm clean, but this is your call."

He gripped her hips, whether to hold her away or encourage her to hurry and make up her mind, she didn't know. But she was sure of this, of him.

Without a word, she lowered herself and joined their bodies. His groan of approval had her smiling as she rested her hands on either side of his head. Matt nipped at her lips before pushing her back up.

"I want to watch every second of this," he murmured.

He might have seduced her, not that she'd put up too much of a fight, but he was handing over total control. Matt wasn't a man who liked to give up his power…which just proved how much he wanted her, wanted *this* to happen.

Rachel would have to analyze that from all different directions later. Right now, she only wanted to feel—and she certainly felt.

Matt's hands roamed from her hips to her breasts and back down. She shifted against him, finding that perfect rhythm. Never once did she shy away from his hot, molten gaze. She couldn't pinpoint that look in his eyes; she couldn't figure out what he saw when he stared at her so intently. But she did know she'd never felt like this, and she wasn't so sure she wanted this to end.

Matt tightened his hold on her as his hips pumped

faster beneath her. That strong jawline of his clenched. Rachel leaned over him, her wet hair falling around to curtain them as she covered his mouth.

Then the dam burst. Matt's hands were all over her as he pushed up to a seated position. Her legs curled around his back and her hips continued to rock against his. When the climax spiraled through her, Rachel tore her mouth away, clutched onto his shoulders and arched back.

He murmured something, but she couldn't decipher the words. She clung to him as wave after wave crashed over her. Before she came down from her high, Matt was clutching her against him, his hips stilled beneath her as his entire body tightened and he let the passion consume him, too.

Rachel circled her arms around his neck and buried her face against his moist, heated skin. As Matt's body relaxed, his fingertips started trailing up and down her back. She couldn't lift her head, couldn't face him.

What had they just done? Part of her mind said they'd both betrayed Billy, but the other part wondered how the hell she could ever be with another man after the way Matt made her feel.

At some point, she'd have to face him. More so, she'd have to come to grips with how this changed every emotion she had toward her best friend.

Nine

Matt had known she wouldn't want to talk. He'd sensed her emotional disconnect the moment their bodies calmed, even while she was still wrapped around him. They'd still been joined physically, but she'd checked out mentally.

What did he think would happen? That she'd flash that wide smile at him and ask him to take her back to the house for an encore?

Sex with Rachel was everything he'd ever wanted… and nothing like what he expected. No fantasy could've compared to having the real thing.

He stood in his living room and waited on her to dress. They'd walked back to the beach house in awkward silence and he'd given her that gap she'd obviously needed. Knowing Rachel, she was trying to analyze her new feelings, was trying to figure out if she'd just done something morally wrong against her late husband.

Matt had loved Billy like a brother, but Billy was gone. Life moved on and he was done waiting. He was done letting guilt consume him. But where did that leave the two of them?

As soon as they'd reached the house, Matt had taken her soaking-wet clothes and put them in his dryer. He'd told her to go shower in the master bath, which was a wall of one-way windows that overlooked the ocean. Surely the combination of the breathtaking view, the rain head and six jets would relax her.

He'd taken his shower outside surrounded by the lush tropical plants he'd had arranged perfectly to ensure privacy for guests…not that he'd invited anyone here. Galloway Cove was his haven, his private life away from the office and its demands.

Rachel was the only woman he'd ever brought here, and damn it if he didn't like seeing her walk around his private domain. There had never been a doubt in his mind who he would bring here. Having shown her his favorite spot on the island, having made love to her with the waterfall in the background…

Matt turned from the windows and curbed his desire. There was no way he could go into that bathroom and show her just how amazing they were together. She knew. He'd seen that look of passion, desire and want staring back at him earlier.

But she'd been in the bathroom nearly an hour. Her clothes had dried and he'd laid them on his king-size bed. Her delicate bra and that dress that drove him out of his mind were displayed for her to see. He owed her a pair of panties, though.

Matt pulled out his cell and attempted to clear his head by checking work emails. His partner had forwarded one where another firm had showed interest in buying them both out. He wasn't sure how he felt about that. True he wanted...hell, he wasn't sure *what* he wanted. He knew something was missing, and as soon as he could put his finger on that, he'd be better-off.

Selling his share of the company? He'd given his partner the chance to buy his half. But was Eric wanting to sell his own, as well? That was definitely something they'd have to discuss via phone because Matt wasn't about to email all of his thoughts.

Shuffling feet down the hallway had him shoving his phone and his business predicament aside. With his body still humming from being with Rachel, work wasn't relevant right now.

Never in his life had he ever put a woman, put *anyone*, ahead of his career. That's how he'd gotten to where he was, able to take off whenever he wanted, travel wherever, buy anything. Yet all of that still left him with an aching void.

And the only time he'd felt whole was when he was inside Rachel.

Raking his hands over his face, Matt blew out a sigh and wished like hell he could get a grasp on his emotions. He'd wanted Rachel physically for years. What the hell was all this other stuff jumbling up his mind for? He couldn't feel whole with her. She wasn't the missing link. Hell, he'd avoided her for a year to dodge all of the other mess that he worried would come with getting this close to her.

But he didn't have regrets about the waterfall, and he'd only just sampled her. He wanted more.

Rachel appeared at the end of the hall. Her steps stalled as she met his gaze from across the room. With her long blond hair down around her shoulders, her dress clinging to her luscious curves like before, he couldn't prevent the onslaught of a renewed desire even though he'd had her only a short time ago.

She looked the same, yet everything was different. If he wanted to get anywhere with her, to convince her that what they did was not wrong—but *inevitable*—he'd have to try to get her to open up.

"Do you want to talk, or just get on the plane and pretend like nothing happened?" he asked, knowing full well he'd never let her forget. What had happened here today was nothing short of phenomenal.

"I'd say it's best for both of us if we go back."

He started closing the gap between them, totally ignoring the way her eyes widened as he drew closer. "To Royal or to just being friends?"

Rachel tipped her chin, but never looked away. "Both."

"We'll talk on the plane."

He started to reach for her, but she held her hands up and stepped back. "There's nothing to say. I was selfish and took what I wanted. We can't do it again."

Did she honestly think he'd let her just brush him aside like that? If she had feelings she wanted to suppress, well, that was her problem, but she was not going to pretend like he was nothing more than a cheap fling.

Damn it. Since when did he get so emotionally invested? He did flings; he did one-night stands. He moved on with a mutual understanding. But now? Rachel was a complete game changer for him and he had no clue how to proceed from here.

"Listen, I'm just as freaked out." He reached for her, grabbing hold of her shoulders before she could move away again. "You think I don't have feelings about what happened? You think I don't know you well enough to realize you're thinking you betrayed Billy? That we did something wrong?"

Rachel glanced away, but Matt took his thumb and forefinger and gently gripped her chin, forcing her gaze back to his. "I don't know if you're more upset over Billy or the fact that you slept with me. You're allowed to feel again, Rachel. I've wanted—"

"I know what you want." She jerked out of his hold. "I don't want to keep talking about it."

"FAST FIVE" READER SURVEY

Your participation entitles you to:
✳ 4 Thank-You Gifts Worth Over $20!

Complete the survey in minutes.

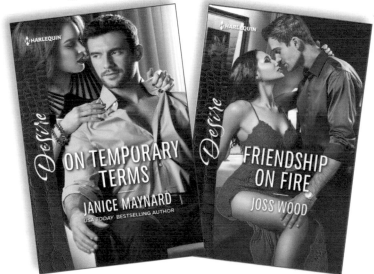

Get 2 FREE Books

See inside for details.

Dear Reader,

Since you are a lover of our books, your opinions are important to us... and so is your time.

That's why we made sure your **"FAST FIVE" READER SURVEY** can be completed in just a few minutes. Your answers to the five questions will help us remain at the forefront of women's fiction.

And, as a thank-you for participating, we'd like to send you **4 FREE THANK-YOU GIFTS!**

Enjoy your gifts with our appreciation,

Pam Powers

To get your
4 FREE THANK-YOU GIFTS:

✳ Quickly complete the "Fast Five" Reader Survey
and return the insert.

"FAST FIVE" READER SURVEY

1	Do you sometimes read a book a second or third time?	○ Yes ○ No
2	Do you often choose reading over other forms of entertainment such as television?	○ Yes ○ No
3	When you were a child, did someone regularly read aloud to you?	○ Yes ○ No
4	Do you sometimes take a book with you when you travel outside the home?	○ Yes ○ No
5	In addition to books, do you regularly read newspapers and magazines?	○ Yes ○ No

YES! I have completed the above Reader Survey. Please send me my 4 FREE GIFTS (gifts worth over $20 retail). I understand that I am under no obligation to buy anything, as explained on the back of this card.

225/326 HDL GM3T

FIRST NAME	LAST NAME

ADDRESS

APT.#	CITY

STATE/PROV.	ZIP/POSTAL CODE

◄ If offer card is missing write to: Reader Service, P.O. Box 1341, Buffalo, NY 14240-8531 or visit www.ReaderService.com ◄

BUSINESS REPLY MAIL
FIRST-CLASS MAIL   PERMIT NO. 717   BUFFALO, NY

POSTAGE WILL BE PAID BY ADDRESSEE

READER SERVICE
PO BOX 1341
BUFFALO NY 14240-8571

NO POSTAGE
NECESSARY
IF MAILED
IN THE
UNITED STATES

"Well, too damn bad," he threw back. "You deserve to know that I've wanted you for years."

Those bright eyes widened in shock. "Don't say that, Matt. You don't mean it."

"Like hell I don't. I've wanted you since I saw you at that party, before Billy interrupted us talking."

"So you just…what? Stepped aside and let your buddy ask me out? You let him *marry* me? You couldn't have wanted me that bad."

She had no idea. Hell, he wasn't sure he'd had any clue until he'd tasted her. Now he only wanted more. He'd had years to process this, but clearly Rachel was just now getting used to the idea of them being together.

Matt crossed his arms over his chest and took a step back. "Go get on the plane, Rachel."

"What?" she whispered.

"We're done here. I've given you enough to think about."

"No damn kidding." She threw her arms wide. "You've confused me, made me face things I never thought about before…what the hell do you want from me, Matt?"

Honesty was the only way. From here on out, he had to let her into his thoughts. She deserved that much.

"I don't know," he murmured. "I wanted you and thought maybe that would be the end of it…but I'm not done with you, Rach. Not even close."

Tears welled up in her eyes as her lips thinned. "I

don't want a relationship. I've got a baby, a degree to finish, a life to figure out..."

"I'm not looking for long-term, either. I just know I couldn't take another day without you. I'm not sorry for what happened and I wish like hell neither were you."

"I never said I was sorry it happened."

Matt turned and headed toward the door. "You didn't have to."

"What are you going to be for the TCC Halloween party?" Alexis asked, smiling and waving around the invitation.

Rachel glanced up from the images of Matt covering her computer screen. For the past day she'd stared at these, not knowing which one to choose for the bachelor auction.

The petty, selfish side of her wanted to choose the worst one, but the realistic side had to admit there wasn't a single bad picture in the lot. He flashed that panty-melting sexy smile in each and every one. Not once had he blinked in an image. He was game on the second she'd started snapping.

"Rachel?"

She clicked to minimize the screen before she turned her focus to her friend.

"The party?" she asked. "Um, I hadn't thought about it. I saw the invitation on the kitchen island yesterday."

Before she'd left, before her entire life had changed.

Before she'd boldly slept with her friend without putting up much of a fight. Despite what Matt thought, she wasn't sorry.

"Are you alright?" Alexis dropped the invitation to her side and stepped on into the office. "I didn't see you much yesterday evening, and the cook said you took yours and Ellie's breakfast up to her room."

Because she just wanted to spend her time with her daughter and not have any contact with people she had to actually talk to—not even Alexis. Rachel couldn't get a grasp on her thoughts and she hadn't slept. Today she looked like a zombie, and her hair wasn't faring much better.

"I'm just tired, that's all." She attempted a smile in an attempt to erase the worry lines between her friend's brows.

"Is the auction becoming too much?" Alexis took a seat on the leather sofa next to the desk. "Dad said he's got Austin starting on the landscaping and gazebo area. I can't wait to see how that turns out. Is there something I can do to lighten your load? Why don't you let me take care of Matt's pictures and getting them printed and ready?"

"No!" She hadn't meant to shout her answer. "No," she said more softly. "I've got it. I think I've narrowed it down to what we need."

She had to go with the one of him in the waterfall. The one right before he'd demanded she come into the water, the one where his eyes had started getting all heavy-lidded and molten with desire.

No woman could resist that—obviously she hadn't been able to. Isn't that what she wanted? Women to throw more money toward the charity? Alexis and Gus were counting on a big check, and Rachel was here to help.

So she'd offer up the man she wanted. There was no denying she wanted him again, and he'd made things perfectly clear he wanted her just as much. But they couldn't sleep together again. She couldn't even look at him on the plane ride home, let alone undress for him again.

Guilt had accompanied her onto the plane. Granted she and Billy had had a rocky relationship, she'd suspected infidelity and he'd pushed her away after discovering the pregnancy. Still, she had been willing to work on their marriage.

But then they'd had that terrible fight and then the accident…and then it was too late to fix their marriage.

"What's going on?" Alexis asked, easing forward on the edge of the sofa.

Even though Alexis was her best friend, Rachel didn't want to get into the events of yesterday. She had to try to figure out how to wrap her own brain around it first.

"I just want to make sure I get everything perfect for the auction," she stated, which was the truth.

Alexis raised her brows and tipped her head. "You're a terrible liar."

So Matt had told her more than once.

"I'm just dealing with a few things," she told her friend. "Nothing to worry about. I'm just not ready to talk."

"Well, I'm here whenever you need me. I can bring wine or ice cream or both. Both is always a good answer."

Rachel smiled. "Thanks. I know you're here for me."

With a nod toward the computer, Alexis came to her feet. "Pull those back up and let's see what we're dealing with. Because from the little bit I could see when I walked in, your Matt is one devastatingly handsome man."

"He's not mine."

Alexis made a sound of disagreement as she came around the desk and clicked on the mouse. "Wowza. Do you see how this man is looking at you?"

Rachel clenched her teeth and stared at the multiple images as Alexis scrolled through. "He's looking at the camera."

"He's looking like he wants to devour you." Alexis glanced over her shoulder and met Rachel's eyes. "I'll assume this is what you're dealing with. Considering you two were at his private island all alone, I'd say you had a pretty good day."

"His pilot was there," she muttered.

Alexis laughed. "In the plane and paid a hefty sum to keep to himself."

Turning, she sat on the edge of the desk and crossed her arms. Her eyes held both questions and compassion.

"Stop staring at me," Rachel demanded. "I'm not talking about it."

"If a man looked at me like that and I was on his own island, you better believe I'd be talking about it."

Rachel pushed from her seat and shoved her hands in her hair, wincing when she encountered a massive tangle. "I need to go check on Ellie. She's resting."

"You have the monitor on the desk and there hasn't been a noise. Why are you running? Because of Billy?"

Because of Billy, because of Matt. Because the only other man in her life she thought she could depend on had turned out to be...more than she ever thought. Shouldn't she feel guilty simply over the fact that sex with Matt had been more amazing than anything she'd ever experienced in her marriage? Forget the fact that Billy had trusted them both?

Then again, she hadn't trusted Billy. Not in the end. Did he even deserve her loyalty at this point? He was gone and if this were Alexis telling her this story, Rachel would tell her friend there was nothing to feel guilty about.

But still, this wasn't Alexis.

"It's okay to have feelings for someone else," Alexis added. "You're young, you're beautiful, you're going to get a man's attention. What's wrong with your friend, the Most Eligible Bachelor in Texas? Honey, women would die to be in your shoes."

"Then they can have them."

Part of Rachel was glad her friend knew some of what was going on without her having to say things out loud.

"I need a break." She came to her feet and sighed. "What do you say when Ellie wakes up we go shopping? Maybe we can find some Halloween costumes for the party. Which is always difficult because I don't want to be a slutty Snow White or a clown. So…something in between?"

Alexis practically jumped with glee. "Yes. I want to go as a Greek goddess. Care to join me?"

Retail therapy to find a fun costume—sounded like the break from reality she needed. Royal had some adorable little shops, so surely they could find something to throw together. Since the party was adults only, Rachel didn't have to find Ellie anything, but she'd gone ahead and ordered her a little unicorn costume online for trick or treating.

For the rest of the day she wasn't going to think about Matt or the waterfall or the tumultuous feelings she had to face. Unfortunately, those emotions weren't going anywhere and she'd have to deal with them at some point. Damn that man for taking their relationship into unknown territory. She had absolutely no experience with flings or friends with benefits or whatever the hell this was called between them.

But she was certain of one thing. No way could she bid on him during the auction. A fantasy date with Matt Galloway was only asking for more trouble.

Ten

Matt walked through the old farmhouse, snapping pictures and making notes. He'd been here for hours, taking each room one at a time. There wasn't a spot in this place where he didn't see his grandfather or reflect on the memories of the greatest summers of his life.

This might not have been the grandiose spread that Lone Wolf Ranch was, but the small acreage and the two-story home still meant more to Matt than anything. More than his padded bank account, more than his private beach house on Galloway Cove and more than any relationship he'd ever had.

He'd already put a call in for a trust contractor to meet him at the end of the week and give an estimate of turning the whole place into something new. Matt wanted to keep the old elements as much as possible, like the built-ins and the old fireplaces, but breathe some new life into the home to make it marketable. Royal was a hot spot right now, so Matt had confidence the place would sell fast.

As he stepped back onto the porch, a lump caught in his throat. The thought of his grandfather's home going to someone else didn't sit well. Every time he thought of selling, well, he hated it. Maybe once an overhaul happened and most rooms seemed newer he would feel different. Perhaps then it would feel less like his family's farm and more just like a business transaction.

The wood plank beneath Matt's foot gave way and he jumped back just in time to save his leg from going through the porch. The damn thing was falling apart.

He rolled up the sleeves on his dress shirt and bent down to assess the damage. He recalled many times doing repairs with his grandfather. He'd always kept this place in pristine shape, and summertime was when he'd saved up all the projects to work on with Matt.

A few hours plus ruined clothes and shoes later, Matt had the porch torn apart and had found old, sturdy boards in the barn to prop up the porch roof.

He stepped back and pulled in a deep breath as he surveyed his destruction. Damn, even in the fall the hot Texas sun beat down on him. The moisture from all his sweat had his shirt clinging to his back.

Tires over the gravel drive forced his attention over his shoulder. Rachel's SUV pulled closer to his truck as he swiped his forearm over his forehead.

Confused, Matt crossed to her car. He hadn't spoken to her since yesterday and he honestly didn't think she'd come to him. Was she ready to discuss what happened? What it meant to their relationship?

When he got to the driver's side, the window slid down. Rachel offered a nervous half smile.

"Hey, there!"

Matt leaned down and spotted Alexis in the passenger seat. "Afternoon."

"It's evening now," she corrected with a laugh. "Looks like you ruined your clothes."

Matt glanced to his grimy shirt and back up. "Impromptu demo. What are you all doing out?"

"We went to find Halloween costumes for the TCC party," Alexis stated. "You'll be going?"

With a shrug, his eyes came back to Rachel. "How did you all end up here?"

She nodded toward the back seat. "Ellie fell asleep as soon as we were done shopping, so we took the long way home so she can get a little nap in."

There were various routes to get back to Lone Wolf Ranch. Interesting that she would choose this one.

"We saw your truck and pulled in," Alexis stated with a knowing grin. What had Rachel told her friend?

"Alexis insisted I pull in," Rachel corrected.

A whine from the back had Rachel jerking around and reaching toward the car seat. "It's okay, sweetie."

"Let me take her home," Alexis offered.

"What? No," Rachel insisted. "We're going now."

"Stay."

The word slipped through his lips before he could even think otherwise. From the shock on Rachel's face and the glee on Alexis's, he had to assume they were just as much caught off guard.

"Matt—"

Alexis was already out of the car before Rachel could finish whatever argument she had on her tongue. Matt reached for her door handle as Ellie's whines started getting louder.

"This is crazy," Rachel muttered. "I can take my own daughter home."

"You can," Alexis agreed as she took Rachel's hands to ease her from the car. "But let her come with Aunt Alexis. I'll give her a bath and read her a story. I'll even get her to sleep…you know, if you end up coming home late. Or even in the morning."

The little Matt had been around Alexis back in college, he'd liked her. Now he suddenly felt like he had an ally.

Matt couldn't smother his grin or stop the wink in her direction. She merely raised her brows as if they had some secret bond. Clearly they both wanted Rachel happy, which meant in this situation, Rachel didn't have a chance in hell of winning the argument.

The two of them had to talk and the opportunity

wouldn't get any more obvious. Being a business-man, he took every open opportunity to further his steps toward his goals. And Rachel was one goal he wasn't about to get rid of. Now if he could just fig-ure out what to do once he fully had her...other than the obvious need to fulfill.

"Take your time, Rach," Alexis practically sang as she slid into the driver's seat. "Don't worry about Ellie. She's in good hands."

Then Alexis closed the door and Matt reached for Rachel's hand. "Relax," he murmured against her ear. "I won't bite unless you ask."

Rachel threw a glance over her shoulder and rolled her eyes. "I won't ask."

Alexis pulled from the drive and Matt headed to-ward the house, assuming Rachel would follow since she had nowhere else to go.

He started picking up the mess he'd created, car-rying the broken boards around back and stacking them in a pile against the barn. When he came back from his third trip, he laughed at the sight of Rachel still standing in the driveway with her arms crossed over her chest. She merely stared back at him and raised a brow.

"You find a costume for the party?" he called.

"Shut up."

She was crazy about him.

"I'm thinking of going as a fireman...if you want to hold my hose."

Well, that pulled a smile from her lips. "You're a jackass."

"No, but I do care about that frown on your face." He moved closer to her so he didn't have to keep yelling. "Seriously, at this point I'll be going as a CEO because I have no idea what to wear."

"So you're going?"

He shrugged. "Why not? Sounds fun."

"You don't strike me as someone searching for fun by way of costume parties."

He laid a hand over his chest. "That hurts, Rachel. Maybe you've forgotten the time I dressed up as a pirate."

Rachel shook her head and snorted. "That doesn't count. You did it to get into that bar when we went to New Orleans for Mardi Gras. If I recall, that costume garnered you several beads."

He still hadn't disclosed how he'd acquired those, and at this point he figured it was best she not find out. He'd like to garner a few acts to get beads from Rachel. The images flooding his mind weren't so much fantasies now, but possibilities.

"Well, we got in where we wanted and a good time was had by all," he stated. "So, are you going to tell me your costume or not?"

"You'll see it at the party."

Was she flirting? Hell, he had no clue. For the first time in all the years he'd known her, he couldn't get a read on her thoughts.

"Want to walk through?" he asked, nodding toward the house.

Her eyes darted to the ripped-apart porch and the two-by-fours propping up the roof. "I'm not sure that's a good idea."

"There's a back door." He grabbed her hand without asking and urged her toward the house. He'd missed her touch. Even though he'd been with her not long ago, the span of time was still too much. "I'm going to have a contractor meet me at the end of the week and discuss renovations."

"So you were trying to save money by ripping into it first?" she joked.

"Not hardly." He led her to the back, where the weeds had nearly overtaken the back porch. "Watch your step."

After helping her up and safely inside, Matt closed the screen door at his back.

"I'm not going to be doing the actual work," he told her. "I was actually getting ready to leave earlier when the boards snapped on the porch. One thing led to another and time got away from me. Demo is a good source to work out frustrations."

"Maybe you should give me a sledgehammer, then."

Though humor laced her voice, Matt knew she was quite serious. "You're more than welcome to help. You might actually enjoy the manual labor."

She glanced down to her jeans and off-the-shoulder

sweater that showcased one sexy shoulder. "I'm not really dressed for renovating today."

Matt held his hands wide. "Clearly I wasn't, either. You up for a little grunt work?"

What in the world had she been thinking? First, she let her friends steamroll her right out of her car and parenting responsibilities, then she'd gone into the house, and now she was sweating like she'd just run a marathon…which was absurd because she'd never run a marathon. Ever. Unless there was chocolate and wine at the end, and even then she'd have to think about it.

Rachel stepped back and surveyed the upstairs master bath. The rubble around her looked like a Texas tornado had whipped through, but her screaming shoulders reminded her she'd smashed everything to bits.

She hoped like hell Matt knew what he was doing by taking everything out. He claimed some of the things in the house, like the claw-foot tub in the guest bath and the old dumbwaiter, would be kept.

Propping the sledgehammer at her side, Rachel smiled. This had been therapeutic…no doubt about it. Maybe she should take up demo work instead of photography for her hobby.

"How's it g—" Matt stopped in the doorway of the bathroom and blew out a low whistle. "Remind me not to piss you off. You do some serious damage with that thing."

Rachel couldn't help but smile, as she was rather proud of herself. "So, what now? I'm a sweaty mess and apparently I have a sitter. Where else do you want me?"

His eyes raked over her body, instantly thrusting her back to the waterfall and making her realize her poor choice in words.

"I already told you that was a onetime thing," she warned, though saying it out loud was more as a reminder to herself than for him.

"You did say that." He remained in place, but the way his eyes drifted over her again only reminded her of yesterday. "Tell me you haven't thought of what happened on my island, haven't played it over and over in your mind, reliving every moment, just like I have. Tell me you can just be done after one time."

Rachel started to argue, but dropped her head and blew out a sigh. "What do you want, Matt? Do you want me to admit that I couldn't sleep for thinking of you? Of us?"

She lifted her gaze, surprised to find him still in the doorway and not right up on her, crowding her and filling her mind with more jumbled emotions.

"Fine," she conceded. "You win. I thought of every single detail from start to finish and then I rewound my memory bank and did it all again. I've thought of you while I'm awake and you've even invaded my dreams. But you know what? Nothing will come of this. You live in Dallas—I'm probably staying in Royal. You're a career businessman and bachelor extraordinaire, and I'm—"

"A single mother and widow. You've reminded me." Now he stepped forward, but didn't touch her. "You want to know how I see you? As a passionate woman who is denying herself because of guilt and misplaced loyalty."

"How dare you," she scolded through gritted teeth.

"What?" he yelled back. "You need to know what I've kept to myself for so long. Why I stayed away for a year. Why Billy was so unhappy."

Rachel shook her head and closed her eyes, as if she could keep the pain from seeping inside. "Stop it. Just stop."

"I've wanted you for so long." His voice softened, as did her heart at his raw tone. "I watched Billy marry you. I watched him flirt with other women. I watched him disrespect you behind your back toward the end of your marriage. When I confronted him, he told me to stay out of your relationship. When you got pregnant…"

Matt clenched his fists at his sides and glanced down to the floor. He cleared his throat before meeting her gaze again.

"I know," she finished. "He didn't want the baby. We fought all the time. But I wanted her. From the moment I knew I was expecting, my whole outlook on life changed and I was excited to be a mother."

"You're a damn good mom." He smiled as he reached out to her. Cupping her face in his hands, he stepped in to her. "It's time you take back your life. Isn't that your goal? You want to start over? Well, now is the time. You can be a mother, but you also need to move on."

"With you? You don't want a family, Matt. Remember?"

His jaw clenched as he studied her face. "You want honesty? I don't even know what I want. All I know is when I'm not with you, I want you. When I am with you, I want you. I want you, Rachel. Right now."

He crowded her in this tiny room full of rubble. Her body instantly responded—if she was honest, the tingling had started in the driveway hours ago.

"I won't pressure you," he added. "But you need to know where I stand for however long I'm in Royal."

Matt released her and turned, stepping over the mess and back into the master bedroom. Rachel remained still, her skin still warm from his touch, her heart beating fast, her mind rolling over everything he said, everything she felt.

She couldn't deny herself, couldn't deny how Matt had made her feel more alive in the past few days than she had in a long time. Did she want to throw that away because she was confused and scared about the future, or did she want to grab onto this bit of happiness?

Rachel climbed over the mess she'd made. "Matt."

He stopped in the doorway leading into the hall, but didn't turn. His pants were filthy, his dark hair was a complete mess and there was a tear in his shirt on the right sleeve. Her attire wasn't faring much better. They both needed a shower, they both were feeling emotionally raw and they both had no clue where this was going.

There were so many reasons she should let him walk right out that door. But she couldn't do it. Maybe it was time she learned by his example and simply take what she wanted.

"Why is it when I'm with you, my clothes end up ruined?"

Her shaky hand went to the zipper of her pants. As she drew it down, the slight sound echoed in the room. Slowly, Matt turned to face her.

Eleven

Matt couldn't move, he couldn't speak. Right before his eyes Rachel had turned into the vixen he'd always known her to be. He'd gotten a glimpse of her at Galloway Cove. But this, this woman before him doing the most erotic striptease he'd ever seen, took his breath away.

He didn't miss the way her hands shook. That slight uncertainty, even while her gaze had completely locked onto his, only added to his arousal. She might be nervous about her feelings, but she was taking what she wanted...and that was him.

Matt didn't even bother to be subtle when he ran his eyes over every gloriously exposed inch of her. When she stood before him completely bare, there was no way he could keep this distance between them.

"While you're here, I'm taking this." She shook her long, honey-blond waves back and offered a slight smile. "Whatever is going on, it's between us. I know you're not looking for a happily-ever-after, and honestly, I don't think those exist anymore."

Her words stirred something in his soul...something that irritated the hell out of him, but with a beautiful, naked woman standing before him, he wasn't about to start analyzing his damn feelings. There was only one thing he wanted to analyze right now and it was all of this soft, creamy skin exposed before him.

"If you're waiting on me to argue with your logic, you'll be waiting a long time."

Before he could wrap his arms around her, Rachel was on him. Damn, if that wasn't sexier than her standing naked before him. She threaded her fingers through his hair and covered his mouth with hers. Her sweet body pressed against his and he wished he could just get his clothes to evaporate so he didn't have to step from her arms, from her mouth.

"I'm filthy," she murmured against his mouth. "I probably smell."

He trailed his lips along her jawline and inhaled just below her ear. "You smell amazing and you'll taste even better."

Matt stepped back and stripped down to nothing. He wanted her glorious, silken skin against his; he wanted to be one with her and he damned any consequence that would come their way later.

With his hands full of the woman who'd been tantalizing him for years, Matt backed her up until they fell onto the old, squeaky bed.

He realized the mattress probably wasn't the most comfortable, so he rolled, pulling her on top. But when he looked up at her, she was all smiles, her eyes sparkling with happiness and desire.

"This damn thing is a brick," he growled. "Did I hurt you?"

She shook her head, her hair sliding around her shoulders. "It's not pain I'm feeling right now."

Just like yesterday, Matt held on to her hips as she settled over him. Would he ever tire of this view? All these years he'd wanted her, but he'd never thought of what he'd want once he had her…now he had his answer. He wanted more Rachel.

"I'm yours," she murmured. "Do what you want."

She was his. His.

No. That sounded permanent. What they were doing was…

Damn it. He vowed to worry about this later.

Matt sat up, thrusting his hands in her hair as he came to his feet. She instantly wrapped her legs around his waist and then he turned and held her against the wall.

"Now, Matt."

His name on her lips was all the motivation he needed. How long had he waited to hear such a sweet sound?

With a jerk of his hips, Matt joined their bodies,

eliciting a long, low groan from Rachel. Another sweet sound he couldn't get enough of.

Rachel wrapped all around him as he set the rhythmic pace. She fit him perfectly—yesterday wasn't just a onetime epiphany. No woman had ever made him want like this, like he couldn't breathe if he didn't have her, like he didn't want to go a moment without touching her.

Matt reached around to grab her backside and moved faster. His mouth ravished hers as the all-consuming need filled him. He couldn't get enough…and wondered if he ever would.

Rachel's body arched against his; her mouth tore away as she cried out with her release. Matt couldn't take his eyes from her. Rachel coming apart all around him would forever be embedded in his mind.

His climax overrode any thoughts, but he never took his eyes from hers. She stared back at him now, a soft, satisfied smile on her face as his body trembled. Little minx knew exactly the power she held over him…and he wouldn't have it any other way.

Their sweat-soaked bodies clung together, not that he was in a hurry to release her.

"We need a shower," she mumbled, her head against his shoulder.

"If the utilities were on, we could make use of that bathroom downstairs."

He actually liked her soaking wet, wouldn't mind having her that way again. An image of her in his Dallas home filled his mind. He'd been to his island, now to his family's farmhouse. Where else could he take her?

Matt patted the glossy bar top to get the bartender's attention. He needed another drink and he wanted to try to make sense of these chaotic feelings swirling around his head. Wanting Rachel, having Rachel and then being confused as hell as to what he wanted now was tearing him up inside.

No, the answer couldn't be found in the bottom of his tumbler of bourbon, but it sure as hell didn't hurt.

"Hey, man."

Caleb McKenzie took a seat on the stool next to Matt. Caleb was another member of the Royal TCC and Matt had met him while they'd both been here using the TCC offices just a few weeks ago.

"What's up?" Caleb asked.

"Taking a break from work."

He'd been at his grandfather's farm for the past several days doing more demo work. His contractor had come by and they'd gone over each room in detail, but Matt was finding the demolition rather therapeutic. For now, he'd wait on hiring his contractor. Mainly because he was enjoying the manual labor and getting back to his roots. Another reason was that Matt knew his grandfather would be proud of his work, and that was more important to him than anything when it came to the farm.

He ordered another bourbon and Caleb requested

a craft beer. After tipping his Stetson back, Caleb shifted on his seat and rested his elbow on the bar.

"I'm taking a break from wedding planning. Shelby probably appreciates the fact I'm letting her deal with choosing the exact shade of purple for the flowers."

Matt laughed. Caleb had dodged the auction block, but in the end, he'd landed his very own fiancée.

Matt wouldn't be dodging the charity auction, considering he wasn't engaged or looking to be.

"Oh, good. Glad I'm not the only one ready for a drink at twelve-oh-five."

Caleb and Matt turned to see fellow TCC member Ryan Bateman striding toward them. He took a seat on the other side of Matt and adjusted his Stetson.

"It's Friday," Matt stated. "Might as well kick off the weekend a little early."

"Hey, I heard you were the new recruit for the auction." Ryan let out a bark of laughter. "None of us are safe. You've been in town, what? Two weeks?"

The bartender set the drinks down and took Ryan's order. Matt curled his fingers around his tumbler and blew out a sigh. "Yeah, I was added most likely because this guy took himself off the market," he said, nodding toward Caleb.

"I'm a catch," Caleb drawled. "What can I say?"

"I just hope the fantasy date I'm supposed to go on involves steak," Ryan added as he took his beer from the bartender. "Other than that, I don't care."

Matt cared a hell of a whole lot about his fantasy

date. If Rachel wasn't on the receiving end, he didn't want to be with anyone else. Sure he dated quite a bit over the years, but lately he wasn't wanting to get mixed up with anyone else. Besides, he knew exactly what she liked…in bed and out. Didn't it just make sense she bid on him? Damn stubborn woman putting an expiration date on their bedroom escapades…

Would she be jealous if he took another woman out? That wasn't a game he wanted to play, but if Rachel didn't bid, then he'd obviously have to wine and dine someone else.

"I have a buddy who would be a great candidate for the auction," Ryan chimed in. "Tripp Noble. That guy is down for anything."

Matt sipped on his bourbon, welcoming the slight burn as the liquid made its way through his body. "I'll let Rachel know. She's been working hard on the social media aspect and getting the headshots ready for the posters. I doubt it's too late to add another, especially if it brings more money."

"Did I hear you and Rachel were at Daily Grind the other day for a date?" Caleb asked, a knowing smile on his face. "You may be off the market, too, if you're not careful."

Matt shook his head in denial. Their coffee "date" had been their first encounter in a year. So much had happened since then and none of it was about to be shared here.

"I'm not looking for a wife," he explained, shaking his head. "I'm just stepping in to help the cause."

"I wasn't looking for a wife, either," Caleb threw back. "These are the mysteries of life."

Oh, there was no mystery for Matt. He wasn't getting married anytime soon. Maybe one day he'd like a family, but he hadn't given it much thought, and he was too busy now to nurse another commitment.

He tipped back the remainder in his glass and came to his feet. After throwing enough bills down to cover all drinks, Matt glanced between his two friends. "I'd best get back to work."

"Are you using one of the offices here today?" Caleb asked.

Matt nodded. "I'll be here another couple hours." Until he traded his dress clothes for jeans, a T-shirt and work boots and headed back to the farm. He needed to get a call into his partner, but Matt's assistant had told him that Eric was out until this afternoon.

It was time to make a decision on the sale of the business...or Matt's half, anyway. Considering he kept feeling a void in his life he couldn't quite describe, perhaps it was time to start liquidating things that didn't fulfill him anymore—like his partnership.

"I'll probably be here later this evening," he added. "The Bellamy has an amazing restaurant, but I'm thinking beer and billiards sounds more like what I need."

"If that's an invite, I'll be here, too," Ryan added. "I'll bring Tripp."

"Shelby is going to some makeup party, so I'm

also free tonight," Caleb supplied, dangling the neck of his beer bottle between two fingers. "It's been a while since I played pool."

"Looking forward to crushing all three of you," Matt said with a smile.

"You want to put money on that?" Ryan asked, quirking his brow.

"I can get behind that." Matt adjusted the rolled-up sleeves on his forearms. "But don't whine when I take all your money."

The guys tossed back insults as Matt headed toward the hallway leading to the offices. He loved being a member of TCC in Dallas, but connecting with the guys in Royal made him feel even more welcome than at his regular clubhouse.

Royal was definitely a town anyone would be lucky to live in. But he wasn't so sure it was for him. First of all, once the auction was over and he and Rachel ended their…dalliance, Matt wasn't sure he could stay in a town where he saw her every day. Because he was absolutely positive she'd want to stay here for the long haul.

He and Rachel would go back to being friends, he'd go to Galloway Cove until he figured out what he wanted to fulfill him and Rachel would meet another guy and settle down, just like she was meant to do.

Without him.

A heavy dose of jealousy and fear came over him as he realized he didn't want to see her with another man. Hadn't the years of seeing and hearing her with Billy been enough?

So what now? How did he carry on with his life and career and attempt to figure out what was missing? How did he move on like Rachel hadn't touched something so deeply inside him?

Matt had never been this confused, this out of control of his own emotions. And he didn't like it, not one damn bit.

Twelve

Rachel tugged at her dress once more. Mercy sakes. Hadn't this dress been a few inches longer? She'd tried this on at the Halloween shop, but being in a dressing room and getting ready to leave your house were obviously two totally different scenarios.

Ellie was down in the family room playing with the chef, who seemed to be doubling as a nanny lately. Since the party was adults only, Gus and Alexis had both demanded Rachel make an appearance because she was working on the auction. Any way they could talk it up and promote it, they would.

So Rachel stood before the floor-length mirror and tugged at her flapper dress once more. Her only saving grace was the added fringe around the bottom. She just couldn't bend over. Or breathe. Or lift her arms.

Really, what could go wrong?

There was no plan B by way of costumes unless she went as a haggard mother, so Rachel blew out a sigh, adjusted her sequined headband around her forehead, then grabbed her matching black clutch from the dresser.

She did feel a little silly going out with a fringe dress, bright red lips and these stilettos. She should be braless, in her sweatpants and getting ready to give Ellie a bath. That was her routine…save for a few nights ago when she'd been wrapped in Matt's arms once again.

Heat coursed through her and she shivered just as she had at his first touch. He'd been so thorough in their lovemaking—likely because he'd been waiting for so long to have her.

There was no denying that a good portion of her nerves had his name written all over them. He would be at the party and she had no idea how he'd come dressed. No doubt whatever he chose, he'd set her heart beating faster.

As soon as she hit the bottom steps, Mae stood there holding Ellie, who was already rubbing her eyes.

"I really appreciate this," Rachel said, giving Ellie a kiss on the forehead. Well, that was a mistake. Now the poor child had a perfect red lip outline. "Sorry about that."

Mae laughed. "No trouble at all. I'll clean her

up, read her a story and get her in bed. She's such a sweetheart."

Rachel loved how this family had so easily taken them in. The family and the staff. They were all so close-knit, so bonded. That's what Rachel wanted for her daughter, for their new life.

"You look quite lovely," Mae stated, glancing to Rachel. "Is there some young man you're meeting at the party?"

"I'm going to talk up the charity auction." Though if she happened to see Matt, she wouldn't mind sneaking off for a kiss or two. "I don't plan on staying for the entire event, so I shouldn't be long."

"Oh, please." Mae patted Ellie's back. "You're young and stunning and dressed up. Stay for the whole thing. I assure you we are all fine here, and if anything arises, I'll call you."

Rachel smiled. "Thank you. For everything you're doing for us."

"No thanks necessary." Mae started up the steps. "You go have a good time and don't worry about a thing here."

Gus came down the hallway dressed as a pirate in all black complete with eye patch and parrot on his shoulder.

"Well, look at you." Rachel crossed to him and smiled. "You look great."

Alexis came from the back of the house, where her room was, and Gus turned, then glanced back to

Rachel. "I'll be walking in with the most gorgeous ladies there tonight. How did I get so lucky?"

Alexis looked absolutely stunning in her white one-shoulder dress with gold sandals, and gold ribbons holding her hair back. The goddess look definitely suited her.

"We're the lucky ones," Alexis stated, giving her grandfather a kiss on his cheek. "Nothing better than a rogue pirate. Are we all ready?"

Rachel nodded and when she stepped outside, the car had been brought around for them. Anticipation curled through her. Even though she wasn't used to being this fussed up, she couldn't deny her excitement about the party or seeing Matt. Being lovers aside, she was glad he'd come back into her life. She'd missed him. But knowing why he stayed away…well, that still left her confused and a little hurt. She wished he'd been up-front with her, but at the same time, she couldn't fault him. Had he come forward after Billy's death and told her he'd had feelings for her, Rachel highly doubted she would've believed him. She certainly wouldn't have been in the frame of mind to hear such things.

Matt was special. What they had was special. She had no clue where they were going, if anywhere, but for the first time in a long time, she was going to enjoy herself and have a good time.

When they pulled up to TCC, the valet opened their doors and greeted them. Rachel went first and stepped into the lobby. The entire place had been decked out with pumpkins, lights, faux spiderwebs and a witch's cauldron, and the entry to the bar and billiards room had a fog machine to really set the stage and showcase guests as they entered.

Searching the sea of costumes, she didn't spot Matt. There were so many faces she recognized, mostly the men she'd photographed, but disappointment settled in. He'd said he was coming, so he'd be here, right? Besides, she was here to chat up the upcoming auction. That was her main focus.

Rachel maneuvered through the crowd, passing a Queen of Hearts, a couple dressed as Belle and the Beast, and another couple dressed as eggs and bacon. Everyone looked so amazing, and suddenly she didn't feel so insecure in her dress, especially considering the lights were low and there were so many people around. The music blared from the DJ's stand at the far end of the room and there were several people on the dance floor already.

This was definitely a fun, festive party. Somehow, though, she'd lost Gus and Alexis. Rachel sighed and eased her way around people to squeeze into a slot at the bar. A nice glass of wine would hit the spot. She rarely drank, but she'd love to have a nice white.

"Buy you a drink?"

Rachel glanced over her shoulder. Matt had a wide grin on his face and had donned a fireman's costume sans the big coat. The red suspenders over the white T-shirt really accented just how in shape he truly was. Granted she'd seen, felt and tasted those fabulous muscles, but now they were all on display.

"I thought you were joking about the costume," she told him.

He raised a brow and leaned in closer. "Want to play with my hose?"

She couldn't decide to laugh or roll her eyes...so she delivered him both. "That line was terrible the first time you said it. Move on."

"That was pretty lame," he admitted. "But, do you?"

"Shut up."

She laughed again as she turned back to the bar and waited for her drink. Matt ended up with a bourbon and paid for both drinks before taking her hand and leading her toward the opposite side of the room from the music. He found a table in the corner that was empty. A slow song had come on and most couples were dancing.

"You look so damn hot."

Rachel crossed her legs beneath the table and toyed with the stem of her glass. "Thank you. I wasn't sure about this costume, but Alexis refused to let me try anything else on."

His eyes dropped to her lips, her chest, then back up. "Remind me to buy her a drink, too."

Rachel had to admit she was glad she'd bought this costume now. The way Matt looked at her was well worth whatever she'd spent. She hadn't realized she was worried what he'd think until now. Pleasure rolled through her at the fact she might just have the upper hand here.

"That's some getup you have, too."

This fireman's costume was sexy as hell. His dark hair and dark lashes eluded to a man of mystery, but she knew all about Matt Galloway. Knew he'd do anything for her, including sacrifice his feelings for nearly a decade. And she also knew he was fabulous with her daughter and that before ever meeting her, he'd put her needs ahead of everything else.

"I borrowed all this from a friend," he stated, then inched closer as his gaze dropped to her lips. "I've missed you."

Her heart fluttered in her chest. Those three words held so much potential. She wasn't sure what to ask as a follow-up. Had he missed her in general or missed her as in he was just horny? Was there a tactful way to ask?

He curled his fingers around his tumbler and settled his free hand on her thigh. Instant warmth and tingles spread through her. Damn it, she'd missed him, too. She didn't want to get too attached, not in any way other than friends. But when he touched her, when he looked at her, she couldn't help but want so much more.

And that was dangerous ground for her to be treading.

"How's Ellie?"

Surprised at his question, and touched that he was even asking about her daughter, Rachel replied,

"She's good. I'm trying to plan a first birthday party for her and work on the auction, so things are a little hectic. I know she won't remember the party and we aren't even in our own home, but I'd still like to do something special."

"Has she been to a beach?"

"What?"

"Why don't we take her to Galloway Cove? She can play in the sand, splash in the ocean, put her face in a cake if that's what you want. We'll take my jet and there will be no pressure on you to do something extravagant. I can have my staff on hand to do whatever you want or I can tell them to leave us. Totally your call."

Rachel blinked. Was he serious? Spending her daughter's first birthday with Matt on his island seemed way, way too familial.

"I didn't think you wanted more with me than..."

Matt smiled and inched closer, his hand sliding higher up her thigh. "Sex? I definitely want that, but we're also friends. Why wouldn't I want to help ease your worries and spend more time with you?"

Rachel shook her head. "I don't know."

"Think about it."

Now that he'd planted the seed, she had no doubt that's all that would occupy her spare thoughts. Part of her wanted to jump at the chance to take a relaxing, fun trip with Ellie to celebrate her first birthday. But the realistic side kicked in and sent up red flags telling her that might not be the best idea.

Rachel caught a flash of white from the corner of her eye. Alexis headed out a side door leading to the hallways and about a second behind her was a man wearing a black Zorro mask. Interesting. Who was Alexis slipping away with? Rachel didn't need to ask, honestly. Her friend wasn't so discreet at keeping the secret of the man she was infatuated with.

Well, maybe others didn't notice, but Rachel knew her friend pretty well. Whatever Alexis wanted, Alexis would get.

"Dance with me."

Matt came to his feet and pulled Rachel up with him.

"I figured you'd want to stay hidden in the corner and make out," she joked as they headed for the dance floor.

He slid his arm around her waist and whispered into her ear, "Maybe I want to feel that beautiful body against mine instead."

Oh, when he said things like that he made her wonder how she never realized how he'd felt. Granted he'd stayed away from her for the past year because he'd worried about her emotions and his restraint. That right there told her how much he cared. She had been upset at first, and she still hated that she'd missed an entire year with him, but he'd been trying to protect her from getting caught up in more emotional upheaval.

Damn it. She was falling for him. There was no denying the glaring fact staring her in the face. At this point all she could do was hope his feelings started shifting, as well. If he'd cared about her for so many years, then perhaps he would want more.

Rachel sighed. She couldn't get her hopes up or hinge her future happiness on a man who clearly wasn't in it for the long haul. Above all else, she had to protect her little family and do what was right for them.

Before they hit the dance floor, Rachel pulled away. Matt glanced back at her and she merely nodded her head toward the side exit. Once she slipped out, Matt joined her.

"What's wrong?" he asked.

The thumping bass from the music inside pounded through the night. "I don't think it's a great idea for us to be seen dancing together. Talking is one thing, but grinding on the dance floor is something else entirely. You are the main event for the auction."

Her heart ached the moment those words left her mouth. But the truth was he was the big draw, and it was her job to promote the auction and help bring in as much money as possible. Matt Galloway would give some other lucky lady a very nice fantasy date.

"I think we need to call this quits after the auction, too." She had to guard her heart and try to keep some semblance of control here.

Matt crossed his arms over his broad chest, which only went to showcase his perfectly sculpted biceps straining against the short sleeves.

"And why is that?" he tossed back. "You think

whoever bids on me will, what? Steal my heart or make me forget you?"

That was precisely what she thought, but she sure as hell wasn't about to express her insecurities.

"I think that for as long as this lasts, we should enjoy it," she corrected, closing the distance between them. "Then when the auction comes, we go back to Matt and Rachel. Friends."

"Friends."

The word slid out like he had sandpaper in his throat. His arms snaked around her waist and a second later she was flattened against his chest.

"You're bidding on me."

With her palms resting on his chest, Rachel shook her head. "I'm not. You know I'm right about this. The sex is muddling your mind, but I'm a package deal and you're not looking for a family. You're not even looking for a girlfriend, so we need to put a stop date on this."

Or else my heart will get broken yet again.

His lips thinned as he stared down into her eyes. "Fine, but you're all mine until then."

Matt's mouth covered hers. A whole host of emotions swept through her and she couldn't decide if it was because of the kiss or the promised threat of being his. Matt clearly had territorial issues…another aspect that aroused her for reasons she couldn't explain.

Oh, wait. She could. Never in her life, not even with her husband, did she feel this wanted, this valued. Matt made no qualms about his current feelings. But what would happen later? When he was done with the good times and the sex? She had to be the one to put an ending to this story.

Rachel lost herself in his kiss, wrapping her arms around his neck and threading her fingers through his hair. She was a woman with wants and desires, and Matt was all too eager to help her check those boxes. She couldn't stop this onslaught of emotions even if she wanted to.

His hands settled on her ass as he squeezed and had jolts of arousal spiraling through her.

The sound of a car door slamming had Rachel pulling back and glancing around. Nobody had pulled into this side lot. She took the moment to pull in a deep breath. When she glanced back to Matt, he had red lipstick smeared all over his mouth.

Reaching up, she swiped the pad of her thumb below his bottom lip. His tongue darted out and Rachel stilled, her eyes locked on his.

"Come to my suite tonight," he told her in that husky voice that practically melted her clothes right off. "I need you, Rachel."

"I can't. I have a baby back at Lone Wolf Ranch."

"Then I'm coming to you," he threatened. "I have to be with you. So either get Ellie and bring her—I still have that baby equipment from our dinner—or I'll climb up the damn trellis and come into your bedroom."

She had no problem imagining Matt scaling his

way into her bed. "There's no trellis outside my window," she joked, trying to lighten the moment before she stripped him out of this damn costume and begged him for anything he was willing to give.

His hands gripped her backside, grinding her hips into his. "What's your decision?"

As if she had one. She wanted him; he wanted her. This was an age-old song and dance. But nothing about this was typical or normal or…hell, rational.

"You better come to me. Ellie will be asleep when I get home."

"Then leave a door unlocked or meet me out back and sneak me in." He nipped at her lips. "And I'm staying the night."

Oh, mercy. She'd just made a booty call date with her best friend and she was sneaking him into her temporary housing. Classy. Real classy.

Her hormones didn't seem to care, though. The anticipation of the night's events only had her body humming even more.

What was she going to do when it was time to call it quits?

Thirteen

"Where the hell are they?" Gus demanded.

Rose shook her head and sighed. "They've both been missing from the party for nearly an hour."

Alexis and Daniel had snuck out. There was no other way to spin this. They were purposely trying to sabotage the auction and totally go against their family's wishes. Gus couldn't stand the thought of a Clayton stealing his sweet Lex away.

Gus turned back to Rose. He'd sent her a text to meet him in the back gardens on the other side of the clubhouse and away from the party so as not to be seen. He'd gone out and she'd come about five minutes later.

As he stared at her, with the moonlight casting a glow over this elegant, vibrant woman, Gus couldn't ignore the punch of lust to his gut. He'd had that same heady reaction multiple times when they'd been younger, but he couldn't afford that now. Those days were gone, decades had passed. Lives had been changed.

Besides, he flat-out didn't want to feel anything for her. Things were much simpler if he could just go on thinking of Rose Clayton as the enemy.

But she'd come to the party dressed from the Victorian era and he couldn't deny how stunning she was. Even though they weren't together, never would be and he still had that anger simmering inside of him, he could freely admit she was just as breathtaking as ever. The dip in her waist only accented the swell of her breasts practically spilling over the top of her emerald-green dress.

Damn it. He needed to focus and not think of her tempting body…or her at all. One wrong turn in his thoughts and he'd fall down that rabbit hole of memories he'd vowed never to rehash.

"So what do we do?" she asked. "I called Daniel, but he didn't pick up."

"I did the same with Alexis."

Rose smoothed her white curly wig over one shoulder. "On the upside, he has agreed to be in the auction. Just make sure you get your granddaughter out of the way of bidding when he hits the stage."

"I know my part," he growled, frustrated over the missing couple and agitated with himself for that niggling of want toward Rose. "Alexis won't be around even if I have to fake a heart attack."

Rose's eyes widened. "Don't joke about something like that."

Was that…care in her tone? *Whatever.* He wasn't giving that a second thought right now. He had a mission and he couldn't deviate from it.

"I'll text Alexis and tell her I'm not feeling well," Gus stated, pulling his phone from his baggy pirate pants. He hated this damn costume. He'd rather have dressed up as a rancher, but Alexis had forbidden him to wear his everyday clothes. "We came together so I'll have her meet me in the lobby. Surely that will get a response."

Rose nodded. "Good."

Gus shot off his text and held his phone, waiting. Silence curled around him and Rose, and the tension seemed to grow thicker with each passing second. There was so much he wanted to say, so many things he'd bottled up over the years, but what would be the point? Yes, he wanted answers. Hell, he *deserved* answers. But learning the truth of what happened all those years ago didn't matter now. Nothing mattered but stopping their grandchildren from falling in love…or whatever the hell they called it. The thought of his sweet granddaughter hooking up with a Clayton irritated the hell out of him.

Alexis deserved better and he was going to steer her in the direction her life needed to go. If that was meddling, well then he wasn't the least bit sorry. He only wanted what was best for her, and that certainly wasn't Daniel Clayton.

The phone vibrated in his hand. "She's going to meet me in the lobby in ten minutes."

Rose's shoulder sagged a bit, as if she'd been holding her breath. Considering they were both on the same page as to how much they *didn't* want Daniel and Alexis together, he was kind of glad Rose was his partner in crime here.

"I'll slip out and go back to the party," she told him. "Don't come out yet."

"I know how to do this," he snapped.

Rose jumped and guilt instantly flooded him. Damn it. Working with her was just supposed to be a way of keeping their families distanced for good. Instead, the more time he spent with her, the more his mind kept playing tricks on him and making him believe he was intrigued once again by her.

But that was absurd. Rose had been his first love; it was probably some residual emotions that had simply never gone away. He simply hadn't been around her this much in…well, decades. That's all. He was just mesmerized and captivated momentarily by her timeless beauty and her tenacity. Then he remembered it was that beauty and tenacity that had pulled him in and spat him out so long ago.

"Good night, Rose."

He dismissed her, feeling like an ass but needing to get out of here. Just as he started to pass, Rose reached out and put her hand on his arm. Gus stiffened at her unexpected touch. He didn't look over at her—he couldn't.

"We don't have to be enemies," she murmured softly.

Gus swallowed and fisted his hands at his sides. Nothing he said at this point would be smart. What could he say? They were enemies, after all, and that was all on her.

Choosing to remain silent, he kept his eyes on the exit and walked away. Whatever was going through her mind, he didn't want to know. They couldn't get distracted by anything, sure as hell not each other.

Gus pushed Rose from his mind and headed toward the lobby. He had to get Alexis out of here and away from Daniel. There wasn't a doubt in his mind that the two had snuck off together. If his granddaughter knew he had concocted the auction to keep her away, she'd never forgive him. Which was why she could never find out and why he needed to limit his face-to-face time with Rose.

And that was just one of the many reasons he had to curtail his alone time with the woman who had once crushed him.

How long should she wait? More importantly, why had she agreed to this preposterous plan of letting Matt into Lone Wolf Ranch?

Rachel sat on the back porch swing and blew out a sigh. She hadn't agreed—not in words, anyway. She'd kissed and groped all over the man instead. Clearly giving him the silent answer he wanted.

Clutching the baby monitor, Rachel pushed off the floor of the porch with her toe to set the swing in motion. There was something so calming, so soothing about country life. To hear the crickets, to see the bright stars, to know that your neighbor wasn't right on top of you was so freeing, and she valued the privacy. She really should start looking for a home of her own. She loved Royal and knew now with 100 percent certainty that she'd be setting her roots here. Ellie would love the park, love the farms, the community.

Rachel couldn't deny she also wanted a bit of distance from her in-laws. First, they'd wanted her to move in with them so they could care for her and Ellie. Then they'd wanted her to let Ellie stay there so Rachel could finish school and find a home. Her mother-in-law had called this evening, but Rachel had let it go to voice mail. She knew they meant well, and understood that they would forever grieve Billy's death, but when Rachel spent any time with them, she got sucked into that black hole, and she couldn't afford that…not if she wanted to move on to the life she and her baby needed.

An engine caught her attention and for a split second Rachel thought Matt was here. But the headlights and sound came from the direction of the barn where the hay was stored.

Confused, Rachel kept her gaze on the vehicle as it slowly came down the drive toward the exit. There was no mistaking that truck. She'd seen it before.

As the vehicle passed the house, she got a glimpse of a profile and, yup. That was definitely Daniel Clayton. Rachel bit the inside of her cheek as her gaze went back to the darkened barn. Looks like she wasn't the only one sneaking around to be with a man tonight. Rachel just hoped Matt wasn't spotted by Alexis. That was a conversation she didn't want to have with her roommate.

The low rumble of another vehicle approaching had her heartbeat kicking up. Matt pulled his truck around the back of the house and parked like he had every right to be here. Something about his arrogance—or confidence, as he'd called it—only intensified her attraction.

Why did this have to be the man to get her attention? Why was she able to push anyone else aside, but Matt Galloway demanded her everything and suddenly she had no control? As he closed the distance between them, the shadows surrounding him only added to the intrigue. Considering he'd had a thing for her for years and she'd just discovered it, she wondered if there was anything else he kept from her.

Rachel came to her feet. Without a word, he mounted the steps and she held the door open. Moving quietly through the house, Rachel took his hand and led him toward her own suite she'd been given. Thankfully, it was away from the other bedrooms and large enough to have a sitting room.

As soon as she entered, she turned the baby monitor off, since the crib was in the far corner near the sofa. The bed was on the other side of the suite, but Rachel wasn't comfortable doing this with her baby in the room because…well, because.

She hadn't thought this through very well. Obviously her need for this man had overridden any common sense on the realities of her sleeping situation… not that Ellie was old enough to know if there was a man in her mother's bed, but still.

Rachel held a finger to her lips, grabbed the monitor and urged Matt into the bathroom. She flicked on the light and slid the pocket door closed once he was inside.

"I guess I wasn't thinking that I share a room with her." Rachel shook her head and let out a humorless laugh. "If you want to go, I completely—"

His mouth was on hers, his arms wrapping her up and hauling her against his hard body. Rachel melted. Or, she felt like she had. The more time she spent with Matt, the more she wanted…well, everything.

His hands were all over her at once, stripping her clothes away before pulling his own off. Stepping over the pile of unwanted garments, Matt tugged her toward the wide glass shower. How could she want him this much when she'd already been with him twice? When would this ever-pressing need go away?

Rachel wasn't sure, but she knew she needed to enjoy this while it lasted…because the end wasn't far off.

Fourteen

"Did you have a sleepover last night?"

Rachel glanced up from the office she'd been using at Lone Wolf Ranch. Alexis stood in the doorway with a wide smile on her face.

"Hey, I'm not judging," she immediately added before stepping in and closing the door. "I just saw a truck in the drive before I went to bed, and then this morning I heard it leave."

Ellie held on to her baby-doll stroller and pushed it around before falling back onto her diapered bottom. She'd just started walking, so there were still a few tumbles.

"I'm not the only one who had an evening visitor."

Alexis pursed her lips and took a seat on the sofa near the window. "I didn't come to talk about me.

I'm here for you. Tell me that was Matt Galloway. I'm not even upset that we'll have to take him off the auction block. I'm just so happy you're dating... or whatever."

Off the auction block? Rachel wasn't going that far, and Matt never acted like he wasn't ready to strut his stuff—he just wanted her to bid on him.

Rachel really didn't have any reason to hide her current situation from Alexis. It wasn't like Alexis was going to wave her paddle when Matt came on-stage or run out and tell anyone. She sure as hell wouldn't tell Gus, because her grandfather wanted Alexis to bid on Matt. Mercy, this was one compli-cated web they were all ensnared in.

Besides all of that, Alexis definitely only had eyes for one man, and it wasn't Matt.

"Things are complicated." Understatement of the year. "But, he's still in the auction."

"What on earth for?" Alexis jerked back, almost appalled at the statement. "He's clearly interested in you."

"We've snuck around a little," Rachel admitted. "But, like I said, things are complicated."

Alexis let out a little squeal. "I knew it! And, honey, there is nothing complicated about that man. He's obviously infatuated."

Sex was one thing, her strong emotions were an-other...and she had no clue how he truly felt. All Rachel knew was that he'd be going back to Dallas soon and they'd return to the friend zone. Would he put more time between them like he had before? Because she didn't want to lose him. If she could only have him as a friend, then she'd take it.

Falling in love had never been part of the plan… not that there had been a plan. Every bit of her reunion with Matt had been totally unexpected, yet blissfully amazing.

"You're falling for him." Alexis moved her legs up onto the sofa when Ellie toddled by. "I can see it plain as day."

"Don't be absurd," Rachel denied. She wiggled her mouse to bring her screen back to life so she could finish the social media graphics for the auction. "Matt and I have been friends for years. He was Billy's best friend. He's still going to be the headliner for the auction, so don't worry."

"Oh, I'm not worried about that. Because you'll be bidding on him if he insists on staying in."

Rachel groaned. "Why do you all think that's how this has to play out?"

"You know you don't want another woman bidding," Alexis laughed. "I take it your guy wants you to stake a claim on him, too?"

Throwing a glance over her shoulder, Rachel eyed her friend. "He's not my guy. I'm working on creating a countdown for the social media sites. Don't try to distract me with all this nonsense."

"I think hooking up with your friend several times in as many days isn't nonsense."

Ellie fell over once again, taking the stroller with

her. Alexis eased down onto the floor and helped Ellie back up.

"I am not doing this," Rachel said, turning back to her screen. "But, if you'd like to discuss what happened in the barn with Daniel, I'm all ears."

Silence filled the room. Rachel bit the inside of her cheek to keep from laughing. Daniel's grandmother and Gus had been sworn enemies for years according to the chatter Rachel had heard. The two had once been so in love, but then they'd fallen apart and married other people. There was no way Rose or Gus would want to see their grandkids together.

If Rachel thought her personal life was a mess, she had nothing on Alexis.

"I know you're sneaking around." Rachel clicked on a different font, trying to make this conversation casual to get her friend to open up. "I also know why, so if you want to talk, I'm here."

"Nothing to talk about."

Rachel's hand stilled on the mouse. She didn't blame Alexis for not wanting to confide in her, but at the same time, she wished her friend would talk. She'd probably feel better if she had someone to spill her secrets to. Granted that person might be Daniel right now.

Ellie let out a whine. Rachel spun in her chair in time to see her daughter flop down onto her butt and rub her eyes.

"I guess it's naptime," she stated, pushing up from the desk chair. "Since we both know what's really going on, but we need these guys for the auction, let's just keep this to ourselves."

Alexis stared back at her and simply nodded, which was all the affirmation Rachel needed to know her friend was indeed keeping a dirty little secret. At this point in Rachel's life, she was the last person to judge someone's indiscretions.

Rachel scooped Ellie up and kissed her little neck, warranting a giggle from her sweet girl. Then Ellie rested her head on Rachel's shoulder and she realized there was nothing more precious or important than this right here in her arms.

"You're lucky," Alexis murmured with a sad smile. "I want a family one day."

Patting Ellie's back, Rachel focused on her friend. "You'll have one. Just make sure you find the right guy first."

"You make it sound like Billy wasn't the right guy."

Rachel swallowed the lump of guilt. She didn't want to speak ill of her late husband and she would never say a negative word to Ellie about her father.

"Billy was a great guy," Rachel said carefully. "I think we married too soon and confused lust for love, then expected that emotion to carry us through the rough patches."

Rachel wasn't ready to admit her fear of infidelity.

Alexis stepped closer and rested her hand on Rachel's arm. "Which is why you deserve this second chance. Bid on your man before someone else comes along and takes him from you."

There was no response Rachel could make at this point. Matt was hardly her man, and bidding on him wouldn't secure that spot in her life. Then again, she didn't want to bid on anyone else.

Rachel headed back to her room to lay Ellie down for her nap. Stifling a yawn, Rachel figured she might as well lie down, too. She didn't regret the lost sleep last night. In fact, she'd worried about Matt staying, but having him next to her had only made her realize she wanted him more.

Why had she let this happen? She'd warned herself going in that there was no room for emotions. Matt was the almighty ladies' man; there was no good ending to her getting this invested in their time together. Intimacy had clouded her judgment at first, but now she saw a clearer picture. Did she even risk her heart, her soul, by holding out hope that he'd love her back?

Could she even move on if he did?

The guilt had settled in long ago; at this point she had to remind herself she was young and it was okay to move on. But moving on with Matt? A man who was not in the market for a ready-made family? Maybe not the smartest choice she'd made. He'd never made any indication that he wanted a family life in Royal or that he wanted more than sex and friendship.

Rachel grabbed Ellie's favorite stuffed toy and silky blanket and laid her little girl down in her crib. The first few months of Ellie's life had been rough with trying to get her child to sleep. Between the grief over Billy and an insomniac baby, combined with her schooling, Rachel had nearly lost her mind.

Thankfully, she was on break and Ellie embraced the naps…for the most part.

After placing Ellie in her crib, Rachel tiptoed away and headed toward her own bed. She'd just lie here and stretch out for a bit. She had to meet with the new landscaper who was working at TCC for the auction. He had her list, but they hadn't spoken in person. She'd feel better if she went and discussed her plan.

Her cell vibrated in her pocket. Stifling a yawn, Rachel pulled it out and glanced at the screen. Her brother-in-law was calling. She couldn't keep dodging them.

With a quick glance to Ellie, Rachel eased out into the hallway and slid her finger across the screen.

"Hello, Mark."

"Rachel." He sounded relieved that she'd answered. "Glad I finally caught you. Is this a good time?"

Was there ever a good time when trying to dodge an uncomfortable conversation? She'd never felt a real connection to Mark and his wife, Kay. They were nice people; Rachel just didn't have anything in common with them.

She rubbed her forehead, feeling the start of a headache.

"I just laid Ellie down for a nap," she replied. "What's up?"

"When are you coming home?" he asked.

Home. Right now she didn't have one to call her own. If he meant Dallas, well, she wasn't going back there. No way was she going to stay with her in-laws again. It was well past time she find a place of her own. Not that she hadn't appreciated their help, but Royal felt more like home than Dallas.

"I'm actually helping with a charity auction here in Royal," she explained. "I'm not sure when I'll be back in Dallas."

Mark let out a sigh that slid through the line and wrapped her up in yet another layer of guilt. She hadn't lied, but she couldn't flat out tell him, either.

"We miss Ellie...and you."

Rachel didn't need the added compliment. She knew full well they all missed Ellie, and she wouldn't deprive them of seeing her. She would visit Dallas soon, but she wasn't moving back.

"I'll text you soon and we can all meet up for dinner. I start back to my classes next week and the auction is taking up much of my spare time. But...soon."

That sounded so lame. The struggle to do what was right for her daughter, Billy's family and herself was seriously real.

"We just want to help," he added. "Kay and I... we just want to help you."

"I know," Rachel conceded. "I appreciate it. Maybe you all could come to Royal for dinner one night."

"I'll see what we can do. I'll text you."

Rachel gripped her phone. "Sounds good. Bye, Mark."

She disconnected the call and leaned back against the wall next to her bedroom. Her headache had come on full force now.

Closing her eyes, Rachel willed for some sign to come…something to give her clarity as to what the right answer was for her future.

Finishing her degree and finding a home of her own had to be her next steps. Her feelings for Matt couldn't override that; her guilt toward her in-laws couldn't interfere, either. At the end of the day, Ellie's needs and providing a stable life for her were all that mattered.

Suddenly, she wasn't so tired anymore. She peeked into the room, pleased when she saw Ellie was fast asleep. Rachel rushed to the office she'd been using and grabbed her laptop before returning to her room. She popped a few ibuprofen to help with her headache since she wanted to try to get some work done.

Over the next hour she polished up the multiple ads that would lead up to the auction. There was so much that went on behind the scenes: social media images to create, newspaper articles to write to draw interest beforehand, radio commercials to schedule and so many other things. This was exactly what she was meant to do. Her love of photography would only help her with her marketing career.

She couldn't wait to do this on a regular basis for an actual paycheck once her degree was in hand.

Hopefully she could do some work from home and stay with Ellie. She hated the idea of finding a sitter, but she'd cross that bridge when she got to it.

The phone vibrated again in her hand, causing her to jump. Rachel's pulse skipped as a text from Matt lit up the screen.

Be at my penthouse at 7 for dinner. Bring Ellie.

She sighed. Her headache hadn't completely vanished and she still wasn't feeling that great. She settled onto the sofa in the sitting room of her bedroom. She didn't reply to Matt; he didn't expect one. He wanted her there and they both knew she'd go. Ignoring her need for him wouldn't make it go away.

Perhaps she should just rest while Ellie was still asleep. Perhaps when she woke she'd feel better and would be able to go to Matt's. Their time was limited and every day that passed brought them closer to being put back in the friend zone.

Fifteen

Matt ended the call and resisted the urge to throw his phone across his suite. He'd been arguing with Eric once again, only this time over the price. Matt knew what his 51 percent was worth and he wasn't taking a penny less. It wasn't like he had to sell for financial reasons. No, this move came strictly from an attempt to save his sanity and take the time to discover something that would make him feel whole.

The knock on his door had him jerking his attention toward the entrance. It was twenty minutes after seven, which also had put him in a bad mood because he'd convinced himself Rachel wasn't coming. She hadn't replied earlier and he hadn't spoken to her.

The concierge had set up quite the spread of food along the wall of the living area. Matt had literally ordered everything off the menu and even asked for specialty items for Ellie. He'd done a bit of research on babies to see what she could eat. He knew she only had three teeth, so he ordered extra cheesy mashed potatoes and some pureed fruit for her.

Matt raked a hand through his hair and pushed thoughts of his business woes aside. Rachel was here and he wasn't going to let anything ruin his evening.

As soon as he opened the door, he found himself reaching for Ellie as he took in Rachel's state of disarray.

"What's wrong?" he demanded as he held Ellie against his chest and ushered Rachel inside.

Her hair was in a messy ponytail, her shirt was wrinkly and she hadn't a stitch of makeup. She was still stunningly beautiful, but definitely not herself.

What dragon did he need to slay for her? Because the thought of anything wrong with Rachel did not sit well with him.

"I'm not feeling well." She closed the door behind her and turned back to face him. "I fell asleep while she was down. I started working and the next thing I knew I was waking up, she was gone from her crib and my laptop was still in my lap. Alexis had taken Ellie out and I didn't hear a thing."

She was pushing herself too hard. Trying to do it all on her own, and Matt was done with this.

"Sit down," he demanded. "I'll get you some food."

"Don't fuss," she stated, but still made her way to

the sofa and practically melted down onto it. "You're always trying to feed me."

"Because someone needs to take care of you."

Ellie smacked her little hand against the side of his face and rattled off some gibberish he was pretty sure wasn't real words.

"Has Ellie eaten dinner?"

"Gus said he gave her some pears and Alexis had the cook make some eggs earlier." Rachel laid her head against the back of the couch and let out a frustrated groan. "What kind of mother am I that I didn't even hear her when she woke up or someone came in and took her from the room?"

Matt turned from the array of food and crossed to her. Still holding on to Ellie, he eased down on the cushion beside Rachel.

"You're a mother who is trying to do too much and is going to make herself sick," he chided gently.

Ellie reached for her mom and Matt let her go, instantly realizing he missed the warm cuddles. When had he started craving holding a baby? He'd been so consumed with his yearnings for Rachel, this had crept up on him.

"I just needed a nap, that's all." Rachel smiled to Ellie and smoothed her blond curls off her forehead. "Since someone started walking, I'm constantly on the move."

"When do your online classes start back up?" he asked.

"Monday."

Matt rested his hand on her knee. "I'll hire you a live-in nanny."

Rachel jerked her gaze to his. "You'll do no such thing."

"Why the hell not? You need the help."

"Mae, the Slades' chef, has been helping so much, and I'm not letting you pay for my family."

Her family. She kept him at an arm's length—which was what he'd thought he wanted. So why, then, did it irk him so much right now?

"Billy would want me to help you."

Rachel grunted. "That was a ridiculously low blow."

Yeah, it had been. "You're my friend and I want to help. Don't make this more than it is."

"We're fine," she declared through gritted teeth. "Maybe I should've canceled. I'm tired and cranky."

And not going anywhere tonight.

"Which is all the more reason why you need to be here so I can pamper you."

She slid him a side-glance. "I'm not here for sex."

"I don't always think that's why you want to see me…though I'm flattered to know getting me naked is clearly on your mind."

Rachel rolled her eyes. "You're impossible."

She turned her attention back to Ellie and lifted her up before settling her back on her lap. "Uncle Matt is silly," she told her daughter.

The whole Uncle Matt reference seriously grated

on his last nerve. He didn't want to be Ellie's faux uncle. He wanted...

Hell, he didn't know what he wanted.

In an attempt to pull himself together, Matt made up a plate for Rachel and a small one for Ellie.

"Come to the table," he told her.

Matt took Ellie and sat down with her resting on one of his thighs. "I have no clue if this is okay, but hopefully she'll like what I ordered."

Rachel glanced around at the spread. "I'd hate to see your bill when you check out."

Whatever his bill was would be worth it. He'd buy the damn hotel if he wanted just to make sure Rachel was comfortable and cared for. Anything to make her life easier.

"Talk to me about the auction," he said, spooning up a bite of potatoes.

Ellie put her hands right in the bite, then put her fingers in her mouth. Well, whatever. He'd discovered feeding a baby wasn't a neat and tidy process.

"We added a couple new faces. I'm supposed to shoot their pictures on Tuesday morning."

The growl of disapproval escaped him before he had a chance to stop himself.

Rachel smiled as she stabbed a piece of filet mignon. "Easy there, tiger. It won't end like *your* photo shoot did."

It sure as hell better not or he'd have a little one-on-one with those guys. Jealousy wasn't an emotion he'd ever been familiar with, and he sure as hell didn't want to experience it now. Rachel had made it clear they were back to friends as soon as the auction was over, so he knew he had no right to get all territorial.

"Gus is loving all of this and is constantly looking over the sheet of eligible bachelors," she laughed and shook her head, causing more golden strands to fall from her ponytail. "The two I added today piqued his interest and he's ready for Alexis to place her bid."

Matt gave Ellie a bite of mashed-up strawberries. "Does Alexis have her eye on one?"

"I'm pretty sure there's only one bachelor she's got her eye on, but she's keeping him a secret."

Matt raised his brows. "Kind of like us."

Rachel tipped her head. "Not exactly. Alexis has tried to brush me off when I broach the topic, but she has a thing for Daniel Clayton. They've been sneaking around."

"Why would they sneak? Just because of the auction?"

"The Slades and the Claytons make the Capulets and the Montagues look like playmates."

Interesting. No wonder Alexis had to sneak to see her guy. If Matt didn't have this damn title hanging over his head and hadn't been roped into starring as the headliner for the auction, he wouldn't have to sneak around with Rachel, either.

"Sounds like a mess," he said.

Ellie swatted at the spoon full of strawberries and it flung back onto his gray T-shirt.

"Oh, Matt, I'm so sorry." Rachel jumped from her seat and grabbed her napkin to dab at his shirt. "Let me get that."

"It's a shirt, Rachel. Relax."

There she went again trying to do even the simplest things for other people. She had a plate full of food still, and she looked like she was about to fall over.

"I've got this and Ellie," he informed her. "Your job is to eat. That's all."

Slowly, she sank back into her chair and dropped the napkin on the table. "Sorry."

"Stop apologizing." Damn it, he wished she'd see he was trying to help. "I've got this, really."

Rachel finished eating and Matt ignored the stained shirt and the fact it had soaked through to his chest. Once Ellie was done, he picked her up and grabbed the diaper bag.

"I assume she needs a bath?" he asked, shouldering the bag.

Rachel nodded. "I can do it when we get home."

"You're staying here tonight."

Those doe-like eyes widened. "I can't stay here."

Considering she looked like a soft breeze could blow her over, Matt didn't even consider this a fair fight.

"You're staying and I'll give Ellie a bath."

Rachel smoothed her stray hairs from her face and smiled. "You're joking, right? If you think dinner is a mess, you should see bath time. She loves splashing."

"It's water," he retorted. "I'll live."

Rachel eased her seat out and crossed her arms, leveling her gaze his way. "Don't do this, Matt. I can't…"

"Can't what? Let a friend help?"

"You know what I mean."

Matt shifted Ellie to his other side and couldn't deny his heart lurched when she put her head on his shoulder. How could he not fall for this sweet baby girl? She was innocent and precious and, with no effort on her part, had worked her way into his heart. Perhaps it was because she was his last connection to Billy or perhaps because she was a mirror image of her mother. Matt wasn't sure, but he knew for certain he wanted them both to stay here with him tonight.

"You can supervise," he told her. "Let's go."

Rachel got the water ready to the proper temperature and then started to remove Ellie's clothes. Rachel sank down next to the edge of the garden tub and sat Ellie in the water. Matt grabbed a cloth and a towel and sat next to Rachel.

Ellie patted her little hands on the water and giggled as she splashed herself in the face. Matt glanced for the soap and wondered if there was something special he needed to use.

"I have her soap in the diaper bag," Rachel stated, as if reading his mind.

She stood up and went to the vanity to her bag. Matt kept his hand on Ellie's back, not caring one bit that he was already getting soaked. Ellie's dimpled smile was infectious, and this familial moment was something he'd never thought he wanted.

Did he want it, though? Doing this one time was a far cry from being a permanent family man.

Damn it. He was getting too caught up in his thoughts and letting his heart guide him. He'd never let that happen. If he'd let his heart and hormones lead the way toward decision-making, he never would've become the successful businessman he was today...then again, he wasn't too happy with that job. At the end of the long, dragging days, he still felt lonely, empty. No matter how many mergers he secured, there was still the fact he came home to a quiet house.

Rachel came back with the soap, and after some more splashing and giggles, they finally got Ellie all washed up. Rachel grabbed a spare outfit from the bag and dressed her daughter while Matt cleaned up in the bathroom.

When he turned to face her, he realized her clothes had gotten soaked, as well. He didn't need that clingy fabric to remind him of how her waist dipped in and her hips flared. Those curves were made for a man's hands...his hands.

"Let me get her a bottle," Rachel said, pulling him from his thoughts. "She's going to be ready for bed."

"Why don't you take a relaxing shower or bath or whatever?" he suggested. "Get a bottle for me and I'll get her to sleep."

Rachel patted Ellie's back and smiled. "You're really determined to do this, aren't you?"

Matt reached for Ellie. "I'm determined to make sure you're safe and healthy, so if I have to feed you, bathe your child, make sure she gets to bed so you can rest, then that's what I'll do."

"We can't stay here," she argued, though there wasn't much heat to her voice. "Ellie still gets up at night to eat, and she'll wake you—"

Matt put his index finger over her mouth to silence her. She slid her tongue out, moistening her lips, but she brushed the pad of his fingertip. Heat coiled low and it was all he could do not to forget their responsibilities.

Her eyes widened, clearly when she realized what she'd done.

"I'll be fine," he growled. "Now, get that bottle and let me get her to bed."

Rachel finally nodded and Matt eased his hand away. By the time she came back with a bottle, Ellie had started fussing and was rubbing her eyes. The crib was still set up in the living area, so Matt dimmed the lights. He settled in the leather club chair and attempted to find a comfortable position to get into. Rachel stood in the distance and stared, worry etched on her face.

"Go on to bed, Rachel. I'll stay in here with her."

"I won't win this fight, will I?"

Matt smiled. "Good night, Rachel."

He stared back down at Ellie and wondered how

the hell he'd gotten to this point. He never invited a woman to stay all night, and here he was about to spend his second night with Rachel because he couldn't bear to be away from her. He was getting her child to sleep like some fill-in dad. What the hell kind of poser was he? This wasn't what he'd meant to do. He never wanted to fill Billy's shoes.

Billy. His best friend and the man who had been cheating on his wife just before his death. The secret weighed heavy on Matt's mind. Rachel deserved to know, but on the other hand, why would he want to put her through more pain?

He didn't like lying by omission to her. He also didn't like the way his entire life was turning on its axis because he didn't even recognize himself anymore.

Most Eligible Bachelor in Texas was now playing house with a woman he shouldn't want, but couldn't seem to be without.

He was so screwed.

Sixteen

Rachel hadn't spent the night with any man other than Billy, but waking in Matt's bed didn't fill her with regret. If anything, she felt…complete. Having Matt take care of her when she felt bad, having him not mind looking after Ellie one bit only made Rachel fall for him even more.

She rolled over and checked her phone and was shocked to see it was well after nine. She'd missed a text from Billy's mother, but she'd answer her in a bit.

Rachel flung the covers back and rushed out to the living room. "I am so sorry—"

She stopped short when she spotted Matt reclined in the corner of the L-shaped sofa. He had pillows propped around him, Ellie sound asleep on his chest and his head tipped back against the cushions. He was completely out.

Well, if that didn't make her heart take another tumble, nothing would. She knew the friend side of Matt, the one that joked and was always there to lend a hand. Then she'd discovered the deliciously sexy side of him when he'd taken their relationship to a new level.

But seeing him hold her child, mimicking the role of a father, had her questioning just how deep she'd gotten with him. How could she ever reverse such strong feelings? Love was about as deep as it went, and there was no magical switch to just turn it off.

Rachel tiptoed toward them, but Matt stirred. He blinked a few times before focusing on her. A sleepy smile spread across his gorgeous face. This was the sexy side, the side she would never tire of seeing. She only wished they could take the day and spend it in his bed, forgetting the world and doubts and fears.

"She got up really early," he whispered. "I tried not to wake you, but I guess we fell back asleep."

"How early, and why didn't I hear her?"

Matt shifted, holding on to Ellie as he sat up a little more. "I was up working and it was around five."

Good grief. Here she'd slept like the dead and hadn't even noticed. That was the second time in as many days.

"Are you feeling better?" he asked softly.

Rachel nodded. "I can't believe I slept that long."

"You clearly needed it."

Ellie started squirming and Rachel stepped forward. "Let me take her."

Before she could reach her, Rachel's cell vibrated in her hand. She glanced down and frowned at the second message from Billy's mother.

"Everything okay?"

"Billy's family wants to come visit since I'm not getting back to Dallas fast enough," she sighed and sank down onto the couch next to Matt, taking Ellie from his chest. "I haven't told them I'm staying here permanently. They want to take Ellie so I can finish my degree. They've made it clear they can give her a good life."

Rachel kissed her baby on her head and nestled close. "I appreciate the sentiment, but there's no way in hell that's happening. Do they honestly think I'll give her up?"

"Have they seen her much since Billy's death?"

Rachel shrugged. "Some. They've just been hovering, and honestly, they're one of the main reasons I want to move. I can't handle being under their microscope. The calls, the texts—it's all day long."

Matt moved the pillows from between them and leaned in closer. His rumpled hair and the baby food on the shoulder of his T-shirt made him look like the opposite of the Most Eligible Bachelor in Texas. Yet he'd never looked hotter or more desirable. And she knew she was treading some very dangerous water here. Not only had she opened her heart to him, she'd let him in with her daughter, and that was an image Rachel would never be able to erase.

"Ellie is their only link to Billy," Matt said, resting his hand on her knee. "They just don't want to lose everything. Maybe you guys could come to some sort of visitation schedule that works for everyone."

"Mark and his wife asked me for full custody. Can you believe that?"

Matt shook his head. "Clearly that's a no, so sit down and talk with them. Tell them you'll be living here and see about letting them come to see Ellie. This doesn't have to be ugly, and it shouldn't be a fight. If you need, I have an excellent attorney I keep on retainer."

Rachel shook her head. "No. You're right. We can work through this. I'll call her in a bit."

When Ellie perked up and glanced around the room all bright eyed, Matt laughed. "At least she wakes up pleasant."

"She's usually a happy baby. I'd better call down and order some breakfast."

"I actually need to head over to the farmhouse and get a few things done," he told her as he came to his feet. "How about you meet me for lunch in town at the Royal Diner around one?"

Rachel smiled. "I'd love to. Are you sure you don't want me to order you something?"

He leaned down and kissed her. "I want you to

stay as long as you like. In fact, why don't you stay with me while I'm in town? I want you in my bed, Rachel."

As much as she'd love to stay in his bed each night, she couldn't for so many reasons. Though that heated look he pinned her with had her questioning those reasons.

"If word got out that I was sleeping here with you, how well do you think that would go over at the auction?"

He stood straight up and cocked his head, smiling wide. Her toes curled and her belly tingled. "The auction where you'll bid on me and then take me home to have your wicked way with me?"

Rachel rolled her eyes and extended her leg to kick him slightly on his thigh. "Get out of here and take that ego with you."

But that's exactly what she wanted and he damn well knew it.

Holding on to her baby, Rachel eased to the corner of the sofa Matt had just vacated. She couldn't contain the smile and she wasn't even going to try. Maybe she would bid on him, but she had limited funds and probably wouldn't be able to compete with the other women of Royal and the surrounding area.

But what if she did bid and win? Then, when the auction was over, she'd tell him how she truly felt. If she had learned anything from Billy's death it was that tomorrow wasn't promised. Rachel never thought she'd feel such a strong pull toward another man, but everything she had inside her for Matt was completely different than her feelings for Billy.

And maybe she'd just have to let him in on her little secret.

Gus and Alexis had taken Ellie to the park for a picnic and to play. Rachel figured it was because there was a bit of tension swirling between the two Slades over the auction, but Rachel had her own issues to worry about.

She pulled up early to meet Matt at the diner. With a deep breath, she pulled out her phone and dialed her mother-in-law. Matt was right…the sooner she discussed this situation, the better off everyone would be. It wasn't fair to deprive Ellie of her grandparents. They obviously loved her, and that was at least the mutual ground they'd need to build from.

The phone rang twice before Alma Kincaid answered. "Hello?"

"Alma? Um, it's me. Is this a good time?"

"Rachel," the woman practically squealed. "Of course, of course. How are you? How's our sweet Ellie-bug?"

Rachel gripped her cell and watched as a family of four went into the restaurant. "We're all doing great. I'm sorry I missed your calls. These past couple weeks have been busy. I'm working on a charity auction and I start back to class on Monday. My last semester before I earn my degree."

"That's wonderful," Alma praised. "You sound so swamped, though. Ellie is more than welcome to stay with me until your load lightens."

"That's one of the reasons I called to talk to you." *Please, please let this go smoothly.* "I know you guys miss Ellie and I'd like to see if we can come to some sort of agreement on a visitation schedule. My plan is to move to Royal…for good."

"For good?" Alma repeated. "Well, um, okay. I wasn't expecting that. But, I understand staying in Dallas might bring back some painful memories. Billy's death changed us all."

Wasn't that the truth?

"I'm just so thrilled you're going to let us see her," Alma went on. "I was so worried after he died that you'd shut us out. I tried to talk him out of going to that divorce lawyer and told him to work on your marriage. I mean, you were pregnant, and that certainly was not the time to end things."

Stunned, Rachel stared at the American flag flapping in the wind across the street at the courthouse. "Divorce lawyer?"

"I couldn't believe it myself," she added, oblivious to the bomb she'd just dropped. "But I love Ellie and I love you like my own, Rachel. I would love to come up with a visitation schedule. Whatever works best for you and Ellie. I'm willing to drive to Royal as often as I can."

Suddenly shaking, Rachel couldn't think. Billy had been ready to divorce her? She knew they'd been arguing, that they'd started growing apart, but that word had never been thrown around.

"Alma, I need to call you back. Will you be home this evening?"

"Of course, dear. It's so good to hear from you. Give Ellie-bug a kiss from Gran."

Rachel disconnected the call and rubbed her forehead. Pulling in one deep breath after another, she willed her breathing to slow.

The tap on her window had Rachel jerking in her seat. Matt stood outside her car with a smile on his face and opened her door.

When she slid out and looked up at him, his smile vanished. "What happened? Is it Ellie? Are you feeling bad again?"

She was feeling bad, almost nauseous, in fact. "I just got off the phone with Alma."

Matt's brows drew in. "Did she not agree to your idea? I can call my lawyer now—"

"No. We didn't even get to discuss the schedule. She was just glad I was letting Ellie be part of their life since Billy—uh—had already gone to a divorce attorney."

Matt eased back, his eyes showing no sign of

shock. In fact, Rachel only saw one emotion, and that was acknowledgment.

"You knew?" she whispered hoarsely.

He slid a hand over the back of his neck and started to reach for her. "Listen—"

She slid from between him and the car to avoid his touch. "No. How dare you know and not tell me!"

Matt glanced around when she shouted, then took a step closer. "You don't want to do this here."

"I don't want to do it at all," she growled through gritted teeth. "You betrayed me."

Matt gripped her shoulders and came within a breath of her. Although she wanted nothing more than to shove him away, she didn't. Causing a scene wouldn't repair what had been done, wouldn't piece back together her shattered heart. She'd trusted him. Damn it, she'd fallen in love with him.

For the second time, she'd laid her heart on the line only to have it crushed and her trust betrayed.

"When did you want me to tell you?" he asked, lowering his voice. "I just found out the day he died. We were on the boat and he mentioned it, then I tried to talk to him. The accident happened so fast, then you were distraught from the loss. At what point should I have caused you more pain, Rachel?"

She closed her eyes, trying to force the truth away. Learning her most trusted friend had kept something so pivotal from her only exacerbated the pain he referred to.

When she focused back on him, Rachel's heart lurched. The way he held her, the way he looked at her all seemed so genuine and full of concern. But everything had been a lie.

"You knew this information and then you dodged me for a year," she accused. "I understand not telling me immediately, but did you ever think of reaching out to me after that? Is that why you really stayed away, because you wanted to keep your friend's secret? Did everyone know he didn't want me? Didn't want our baby?"

Damn, this hurt. The idea that she and Ellie were going to be tossed aside crushed her in ways she hadn't thought possible. And the fact that Matt knew and remained silent…well, she had no label to put on that crippling emotion.

"I never wanted you hurt," he ground out.

Rachel looked into his eyes, searching for answers she might never have. "Would you have ever told me?"

Matt's lips thinned as he remained silent. That told her all she needed to know.

"Let me go," she murmured. "I can't do this anymore."

"Rachel." His grip remained as he pulled her against his chest. "Let's go somewhere and talk. You have to know I never meant to hurt you."

"Yet you did."

He rested his forehead against hers. "Don't push me out. Let me explain."

"What else have you lied about?" she asked, her voice cracking, and she damned her emotions for not staying at bay until she was alone. "Did you actually want to be with me, or was this just because Billy—"

"None of this is because of Billy," he demanded. "I've wanted you for years, Rachel. You can't tell me you didn't feel it when I kissed you, touched you. Made love to you."

Rachel started to protest, but Matt's mouth covered hers. Their past kisses had been frenzied, intense, but this one could only be described as passionate and caring. He took his time as he framed her face with his hands. Despite everything, Rachel started to melt into him because she couldn't disconnect her heart from her hormones.

"Perfect."

They jerked apart at the unfamiliar voice. A young woman stood next to them with her phone, taking a photo.

"Mr. Galloway, can you comment on your relationship here?" the woman asked, whipping out a small notepad and pen. "Are you officially not the Most Eligible Bachelor in Texas anymore? And what about the charity auction? Rumor has it you're the star of the show."

Rachel backed away as Matt took a step toward the journalist.

"Delete that image now," he demanded. "And there will be no comment."

The lady's eyes widened as she slid her paper and pen back into her oversized purse, then she turned and ran. Matt cursed as he raked a hand through his hair. No doubt the woman was on her way to post the steamy picture on any and every social media site she could.

Dread racked through her. What had she been *thinking*? She couldn't kiss Matt on the sidewalk in broad daylight. He was the main attraction for the auction. Who else had seen the kiss?

None of this was going to work. She and Matt were nearing the end, and that reporter just solidified the fact. Rachel had a baby to look after; she had a career to get started and a new life to create. She needed to provide stability and a solid future for her and Ellie.

Matt's lie, even by omission, and now the fact she'd be all over social media in seconds…damn it, the forces pulling them apart were getting stronger.

Her mind scrambled in so many different directions. She couldn't stay here. That much she was certain of.

Rachel turned toward her car and opened the door.

"Wait," Matt commanded. "Don't go."

She threw a look over her shoulder. "We're done, Matt. And now I have to go do damage control to save you in this auction."

She settled behind the wheel and started to close the door.

"You can't run from us, Rachel," he called out.

One last time, she glanced up to him. "There is no us."

Seventeen

"The press conference is scheduled for tomorrow evening."

Rachel heard Gus's words, but she didn't look up. Since the debacle two days ago with Matt, social media had exploded. Between the media speculation about Texas's most famous bachelor being taken off the market and the biggest draw for the auction in question, Rachel figured the only way to combat this cluster was to hold a press conference. That way she could field questions and make a statement, focusing on the bachelors for the auction, including Matt, and putting to rest any claims that he was off the market.

He certainly wasn't hers—no matter how much she wished he was.

Rachel put another block on top of Ellie's and Ellie promptly kicked them down.

"Listen, darlin', I know you think your man betrayed your trust, but sometimes men do stupid things in the name of love."

Rachel jerked her attention toward where Gus had taken a seat in the leather recliner. "Alexis told you?"

"She gave the important details." He took off his Stetson and propped it on his bent knee. "Don't be upset with her. She's worried about you and so am I. You're like family to us now."

Rachel couldn't suppress her smile. "You guys feel the same to me."

"As much as I wanted my granddaughter to bid on Matt, I have a feeling he's off the table."

Rachel shook her head and handed Ellie another block. "He's still on," she corrected. "Whatever we had, it's over."

"Because he didn't tell you your husband was going to leave you?" Gus blew out a sigh and eased forward in his chair. "If Matt cared about you even a little bit, he wouldn't want you hurt more than necessary."

Rachel didn't want to argue about this; she didn't want the voice of reason to enter in. Because as far as she was concerned, she had every right to be angry at Matt for keeping the truth from her. Especially after learning that he had no intention of ever telling her. Had his loyalties to her late husband been that strong? Had everyone known Billy was leaving but her?

"I'm sure your mind is racing," Gus went on. "But if you don't listen to anything I say, listen to this. Love doesn't always come around twice in a lifetime. Trust me on that. Very few are lucky enough to get another chance. If you feel anything for Matt, you need to tell him."

Rachel came to her feet and leaned down to pick Ellie up. "Gus, I've come to love you like my own grandfather, but right now I can't handle this. Matt isn't mine, and I'll be sure to emphasize that tomorrow at the press conference. Now, if you'll excuse me, Ellie needs a nap."

Rachel didn't want to sound rude, but she just needed to not talk about Matt or her feelings or anything to do with why she should forgive him. Billy had destroyed her by the hints of infidelity and then rejecting the pregnancy. Now she was going through betrayal all over again with Matt. She never expected him, of all people, to lie to her.

Rachel carried Ellie upstairs and took her time getting her to sleep. She rocked her, sang to her, held her after her breathing had slowed and she was out. Rachel just wanted to hold on to the one person in her life she treasured more than any other.

Finally, Rachel laid Ellie into her crib and went over to the desk in the corner. She pulled up the screen on her laptop, ready to start looking for a home. It was time she pushed forward and made a life for herself and her daughter. Everything that happened before this moment didn't matter. She would finish her degree, find a house and make good on her promise to allow visitation with Billy's family.

But the second her computer came to life, she remembered she'd been working on a large spread with a photo of each bachelor. Her eyes instantly went to Matt. There was no competition as far as she was concerned. The image she'd used of him in the waterfall made him stand out and beg for attention... just like she'd intended.

Only her plan had backfired, and she had to stare at the photo knowing full well that only seconds after it was taken, her life had irrevocably changed. There would be no going back to friends, no matter how much she would miss him. Because, damn it, her heart hadn't gotten the memo that things were over. She still cared for him, still *loved* him. But how could she ever trust him again?

Rachel couldn't look away from the image. The longer she stared, the more mesmerized she became by that dark stare, those heavy lids, that white cotton shirt plastered in all the right areas.

But Matt wasn't just the sexiest man she'd ever known. He'd been her friend; he'd come to her defense in front of Billy more than once when her late husband had disrespected her. Matt had kept his needs to himself for a decade. Who the hell did that?

Were those the acts of a man in love? Had he loved her in that way? She didn't even know how to analyze all of this information without going absolutely insane.

Right now she had to push her emotions aside, no matter how difficult the task might be. She had a speech to prepare and bachelors to introduce tomorrow during the press conference. Damage control was just part of marketing, and this whole situation sure as hell gave her much-needed experience...she just wished her heart hadn't been part of the experiment.

Matt pounded the hammer once more, driving the nail home. He came to his feet and surveyed the brand-new porch and roof he'd spent the better part of two days installing.

And no matter how much demolition or renovation he did of his grandfather's home, nothing had exorcised those demons from him.

Rachel still consumed every part of him. He missed the hell out of her. But it wasn't just Rachel; he missed sweet Ellie. The two females had slithered right into his heart and taken up so much real estate, he had no idea how he'd ever lived without them.

He did know one thing: he'd managed to sell off his 51 percent early this morning when Eric finally came up to Matt's asking price. The weight lifted somewhat, but still there was something missing.

The sale would take time to finalize, but Matt wasn't worried about it falling through. He'd make sure it happened so he was free to move on to…whatever the hell he wanted.

Who knew? Maybe he'd take up residence here in Royal and make this old homestead his farm.

Something akin to a blast erupted inside of him, and Matt's breath caught in his throat. He'd called off his contractor, stating he wanted to do the initial work himself. He wanted the grunt work, the outlet for his frustrations, and a way to get back to his roots when he'd bonded with his grandfather. He would have his guy come in and take over soon enough, but for now, this was his baby to nurture.

He'd brought Rachel here and she'd helped. The most precious times of his life were spent right here in Royal…both past and present.

How the hell had he not seen this before now?

Matt stared up the two-story home once again, now looking at it in a whole new light. He instantly saw the place transformed. He imagined Ellie on the steps playing with dolls and Rachel swinging on the porch with her belly swollen with his child. He saw love and he saw a family he never knew he wanted… but couldn't live without.

Matt checked the time on his cell and calculated. He had just enough of a span to put his plan into motion. There was no way in hell he was letting Rachel get away. He'd waited this long for her, and now that he realized his true feelings, the future he wanted with her, he couldn't let this opportunity pass him by.

She was his best friend, but he wanted more. He wanted everything, and Matt Galloway never stopped until he got what he wanted.

Eighteen

Rachel set her notes on the podium in the TCC club-house. She'd opted to use the back gardens as the area for the auction, and that was still being revamped. She wanted to keep the reveal of the changes a surprise. But she'd peeked in when she'd first arrived, and Austin Bradshaw was doing a fabulous job. She couldn't wait to see the end result.

As she glanced over her notes once more, she cursed her shaky hands. She just wanted to get this press conference over with so they could focus on what was important. The actual charity event. If they didn't bring in the projected goal, Rachel would never forgive herself. She only hoped she hadn't blown it with the whole kiss scene that had been plastered all over.

"All set?"

Alexis came up the aisle of chairs with a wide smile on her face. Her long hair spiraled down around her shoulders and she had on the prettiest floral dress with boots. If she didn't watch out, some man would make a bid for her.

"As ready as I can be," Rachel stated, stepping down from the stage. "It's almost go time. Is anyone out there?"

Alexis laughed. "Honey, this is the hottest thing in Royal and any surrounding town right now. There are hordes of people from several media outlets, plus some prominent citizens outside those doors."

"Well, that didn't help my nerves."

Alexis closed the distance between them and took Rachel's hands. "I figured you'd want to know what you were dealing with."

With a shaky breath, Rachel nodded. "You're right. I'd rather know what I'm facing."

Alexis gave a gentle squeeze. "You know, it's not too late to adjust those notes and have sixteen bachelors instead of seventeen."

Considering Matt hadn't contacted her since she drove away, she'd have to disagree. Not that she'd reached out to him, either. Apparently they were truly over and she'd just have to suffer through the auction in a few months and watch some lucky woman buy him up and whisk him away.

"Whatever we had, it's over." Maybe if she kept repeating those words out loud, and even in her mind, she'd start to believe them. "He hurt me and I just think we started off like Billy and I did. Maybe I mistook lust for love."

Liar, liar.

"You love Matt and he loves you." Alexis dropped her hands. "If you don't bid on that man, I'll bid on him myself."

Rachel smiled. "Well, that would make your grandfather happy."

Alexis tipped her head. "He would be a gift to you."

"Then save your money or bid on Daniel."

Alexis stiffened. "There's nothing going on there. I wish you'd quit bringing it up."

Rachel shrugged. "Then drop Matt and we'll call a truce."

After a long pause, Alexis nodded. "Fine. But you have nothing holding you back from taking what you so clearly want. You might never get a chance like this again."

Her friend turned and headed toward the doors leading into the clubhouse. Rachel closed her eyes and willed herself the strength to get through this press conference. She needed to sound convincing when she laid her claim that she and Matt were friends and the kiss was nothing.

Perhaps they wouldn't know she was lying to save her own ass.

Moments later the loud chatter enveloped her, and Rachel pasted a smile on her face as guests took their seats. This was the most pivotal moment before the auction because she would be quoted. And, to take the pressure off her and Matt and the scandal they'd created, she had visuals of the bachelors to hopefully get the media to focus on the auction and not the infamous kiss.

A kiss she was still feeling. Because no matter how much she tried to ignore her emotions, she couldn't get Matt out of her mind, and every moment she thought of him, her body heated.

Damn man had too much power over her. She fell in love with him easily; maybe she could fall out of love just as effortlessly?

If only flipping emotions on and off were a possibility, she could save herself more heartache.

Once everyone was seated, Rachel glanced toward the back of the patio area as Alexis closed the doors and gave her the nod to begin.

Gripping the edge of the podium, Rachel cleared her throat. "Good evening, ladies and gentlemen. I appreciate you all taking time to be here this evening. I have several points to address, but I promise to keep this short.

"There has been some chatter and misinformation spreading like wildfire," she went on. "I'd like to address that first." She took a deep, bracing breath, then continued. "Contrary to what you may have heard, Matt Galloway is still in the bachelor auction. We are thrilled he's contributing, and not only is he offering up his time for a fantasy date, he's also writing a check matching the winning bid for him."

The crowd murmured and a few clapped, just as she'd hoped. So far, so good.

"The picture of Matt and I kissing was harmless," she added with a fake smile as she lied through her teeth, but she pushed on. "We have been friends since college and he'd invited me for lunch to catch up."

After I'd spent the night in his bed.

"The timing was unfortunate and we do hope this will erase any doubt about him being in the auction. That kiss was meaningless and —"

"Nothing about that kiss was meaningless."

The crowd gasped in unison as they turned toward the back of the patio. Rachel shifted her focus as well and spotted Matt striding down the aisle. His dark suit screamed power and she wished she had her camera to capture that intense look on his face... a look all for her.

Her heart thudded even faster. What the hell was he doing here, and why was he sabotaging her press conference?

He stepped up to the stage and stood right next to her, reaching for the mic and angling it toward him.

"What Ms. Kincaid meant to say was there will now only be sixteen bachelors in the auction because I am removing myself."

"What the hell are you doing?" she whispered through gritted teeth.

Completely serious, he shot her a glance. "Saving us."

All at once, reporters shouted questions and came up out of their seats. Rachel glanced at the hyper crowd and in the very back stood her best friend with a wide smile on her face.

"I will take questions, but one at a time, please," Matt requested with so much dignity and authority, she wanted to smack him for...well this. How could she do damage control and hate him for lying when he was literally standing up for her?

"How long have you and Ms. Kincaid been seeing each other?" one reporter shouted.

Behind the podium, he reached for her hand. That was solely for her benefit, she knew, because nobody could see his actions.

Her heart tumbled.

"Like she said, we've been friends for years. We recently reconnected when I came to Royal for a getaway."

"Are you two getting married? Will you both live here?"

Matt laughed and the low, sensual tone sent shivers of arousal through her. He was making things nearly impossible for her when she just wanted to be angry. Why couldn't he let her be?

"Well, you're jumping the gun," he replied. "I have every intention of asking Rachel to marry me, but I'd hoped to get her alone."

The crowd erupted in cheers and Rachel froze. "You what?" she croaked out.

Matt turned toward her, ignoring the loud crowd. "I want to marry you, Rachel. I want to raise Ellie with you. I want to stay in Royal with you."

He threw those statements out like he was serious. He looked at her like she was the most precious thing in the world. The way he held her hands and waited for her to say something…was he serious?

"Matt—"

"Give me another chance, Rachel. I'll still make a donation to the charity—just name the amount. I love you, and I don't see a future without you in it. Without our family. I want to have more children with you and I hope you'll help me with the farmhouse, because I think it's the perfect place for us."

Well, now he'd gone and done it. Rachel's eyes swelled with tears and she glanced down to their joined hands. "I love you, too," she whispered. "But how can I trust you?"

She realized the room had gone silent. No doubt every reporter had their phones out trying to record this moment, but Rachel couldn't worry about them or what they might or might not put out to the masses.

"I'm terrified," he admitted, resting his forehead against hers. "I've never done love before, but I want to do it with you. There's nobody else, Rachel. You're it. You can trust me with your heart, because I'm trusting you with mine."

The tears slid down and she could do nothing to stop them at his bold, heart-flipping statement.

"I've never known you to be afraid of anything," she laughed. "What about Dallas?"

He tipped her chin up so she looked directly at him. "Nothing matters but you saying yes."

"What exactly are you asking me for?"

That signature heart-stopping, toe-curling smile spread across his face. "Everything."

She slid a glance to the crowd only to find each and every person had scooted closer to the stage. Rachel laughed as she turned back to Matt.

"I need to finish the press conference."

Matt's eyes studied her, but then he took a step back. Rachel turned back to the podium, glanced down to her useless notes and flung them in the air.

"Bachelor Seventeen is officially off the auction block," she declared.

The hoots and shouts were deafening and Rachel squealed when Matt wrapped his arms around her and kissed the side of her neck as he spun her around.

"I knew you'd end up with me." He smoothed her hair back from her face. "I hate to say I told you so, but…"

Rachel wrapped her arms around him and smacked his lips with a kiss. "I don't mind. You're mine, Matt Galloway. My very own bachelor."

He kissed her back, pouring promises and love into each touch.

"As you can see, we've lost another bachelor."

Rachel laughed against Matt's mouth at Alexis's statement to the crowd.

"I assure you all, we will have plenty of available men to choose from," Alexis went on, her voice echoing into the mic. "Rachel prepared a wonderful presentation, but she and Matt will be slipping out, and I'll be taking over and answering any questions."

Matt wrapped his arm around Rachel's waist and ushered her down the steps. They attempted to wade through the aisle, but kept getting high fives and hugs and smiles from each guest. Rachel wasn't sure how she'd gone from explaining why Matt was the greatest bachelor for the auction to removing him and agreeing to be his wife in the span of ten minutes.

That pretty much summed up their courtship, though, didn't it? He'd swept back into her life, dredging up emotions she never even knew she had and then forced her to see this second chance she'd been given at a lifetime of happiness.

Of course, to her this had been fast, but to him, he'd had feelings for a decade.

Once they reached the inside of the TCC clubhouse, Matt pulled her down the hallway toward the offices.

"Where are we going?" she asked.

"I have something for you."

Intrigued, she followed him into the office at the end of the hall. Matt closed the door and went to the desk.

"I brought this with me because I didn't want to

wait." He pulled something from the drawer and turned back to her. "I'm sorry I hurt you, after Billy's death and again the other day. That was never my intention. Hell, Rachel, I'd do anything for you and Ellie."

The fact he always included Ellie warmed her heart. The small box he held in his hand had her heart catching in her throat.

"I didn't want to do this out there," he admitted, closing the space between them. "But I have this ring that belonged to my grandmother. I've had it since my grandfather gave it to me just before his death. He made me promise I would only give it to someone I loved."

Matt opened the blue velvet box and revealed a bright ruby with smaller diamonds flanking each side. Rachel gasped, her hand to her mouth as she tried to control her emotions.

"I know it's not the biggest or the flashiest," he went on. "I'll buy you anything you want. Hell, you wanted an island. I'll get you one of those, too."

Rachel shook her head, causing even more tears to spill down her cheeks. "No. I want this ring and I want your island."

Having something from his past made her feel even more special.

Matt pulled the ring from the box and slid the band onto her finger. "It fits," he said, relief flooding his tone.

"Of course it does." She admired the vibrant red stone. "We fit."

Matt circled his arms around her waist and tugged her against him. "Let's go get Ellie and head back to my penthouse."

"Were you serious about staying in Royal at the farm?"

Matt framed her face and placed a soft kiss on her lips. "If that's okay with you. We can escape to Galloway Cove any time you need a break, but I want you to finish that degree. Who knows, maybe we can start up a company together. What do you think?"

Rachel smiled. "I think we'd be a hell of a team."

* * * * *

Will Gus and Rose succeed in keeping their grandchildren apart? Will the bachelor auction go off without a hitch?

Find out in Million Dollar Baby *by USA TODAY bestselling author Janice Maynard!*

When Heiress Brooke Goodman rebels, her wild one-night stand turns out to be her coworker at the Texas Cattleman's Club! How will she resist him? Especially when the sexy Texan agrees to a temporary marriage so she can get her inheritance and she learns she's expecting his child...

Don't miss a single installment of the six-book Texas Cattleman's Club: Bachelor Auction Will the scandal of the century lead to love for these rich ranchers?

Runaway Temptation *by USA TODAY bestselling author Maureen Child*

Most Eligible Texan *by USA TODAY bestselling author Jules Bennett*

Million Dollar Baby *by USA TODAY bestselling author Janice Maynard*

His Until Midnight *by Reese Ryan*

The Rancher's Bargain *by Joanne Rock*

Lone Star Reunion *by Joss Wood*

COMING NEXT MONTH FROM

HARLEQUIN® *Desire*

Available November 6, 2018

#2623 WANT ME, COWBOY
Copper Ridge • by Maisey Yates
When Isaiah Grayson places an ad for a convenient wife, no one compares to his assistant, Poppy Sinclair. Clearly the ideal candidate was there all along—and after only one kiss he wants her without question. Can he convince her to say yes without love?

#2624 MILLION DOLLAR BABY
Texas Cattleman's Club: Bachelor Auction
by Janice Maynard
When heiress Brooke Goodman rebels, her wild one-night stand turns out to be her coworker at the Texas Cattleman's Club! How will she resist him? Especially when the sexy Texan agrees to a temporary marriage so she can get her inheritance, *and* she learns she's expecting his child...

#2625 THE SECOND CHANCE
Alaskan Oil Barons • by Catherine Mann
The only thing Charles Mikkelson III has ever lost was his marriage to Shana. But when an accident erases the last five years of her life, it's a second chance to make things right. He wants her back—in his life, in his bed. Will their reunion last when her memory returns?

#2626 A TEXAN FOR CHRISTMAS
Billionaires and Babies • by Jules Bennett
Playboy Beau Elliot has come home to Pebblebrook Ranch for the holidays to prove he's a changed man. But before he can reconcile with his family, he discovers his illegitimate baby...and the walking fantasy of his live-in nanny. Will temptation turn him into a family man...or lead to his ruin?

#2627 SUBSTITUTE SEDUCTION
Sweet Tea and Scandal • by Cat Schield
Amateur sleuth: event planner London McCaffrey. Objective: take down an evil businessman. Task: seduce the man's brother, Harrison Crosby, to find the family's weaknesses. Rules: do not fall for him, no matter how darkly sexy he may be. He'll hate her when he learns the truth...

#2628 A CHRISTMAS TEMPTATION
The Eden Empire • by Karen Booth
Real estate tycoon Jake Wheeler needs this deal. But the one sister who doesn't want to sell is the same woman he had an affair with years ago... right before he broke her heart. Will she give him a second chance...in the boardroom *and* the bedroom?

_____

YOU CAN FIND MORE INFORMATION ON UPCOMING HARLEQUIN® TITLES, FREE EXCERPTS AND MORE AT WWW.HARLEQUIN.COM.

HDCNM1018

She was going to be interviewing Isaiah's potential wife.

The man she had been in love with since she was a teenage idiot, and was still in love with now that she was an idiot in her late twenties.

There were a whole host of reasons she'd never, ever let on about her feelings for him.

She loved her job. She loved Isaiah's family, who were the closest thing she had to a family of her own.

She was also living in the small town of Copper Ridge, Oregon, which was a bit strange for a girl from Seattle, but she did like it. It had a different pace. But that meant there was less opportunity for a social life. There were fewer people to interact with. By default she, and the other folks in town, ended up spending a lot of their free time with the people they worked with every day. There was nothing wrong with that. But it was just…

Mostly there wasn't enough of a break from Isaiah on any given day.

But then, she also didn't enforce one. Didn't take one. She supposed she couldn't really blame the small-town location when the likely culprit of the entire situation was her.

"Place whatever ad you need to," he said, his tone abrupt. "When you meet the right woman, you'll know."

"I'll know," she echoed lamely.

"Yes. Nobody knows me better than you do, Poppy. I have faith that you'll pick the right wife for me."

With those awful words still ringing in the room, Isaiah left her there, sitting at her desk, feeling numb.

The fact of the matter was, she probably could pick him a perfect wife. Someone who would facilitate his life, and give him space when he needed it. Someone who was beautiful and fabulous in bed.

Yes, she knew exactly what Isaiah Grayson would think made a woman the perfect wife for him.

The sad thing was, Poppy didn't possess very many of those qualities herself.

And what she so desperately wanted was for Isaiah's perfect wife to be her.

But dreams were for other women. They always had been. Which meant some other woman was going to end up with Poppy's dream.

While she played matchmaker to the whole affair.

Don't miss what happens when Isaiah decides it's Poppy *who should be his convenient wife in*
Want Me, Cowboy *by USA TODAY bestselling author Maisey Yates, part of her Copper Ridge series!*

Available November 2018 wherever Harlequin® Desire books and ebooks are sold.

www.Harlequin.com

Love Harlequin romance?

DISCOVER.

Be the first to find out about promotions,
news and exclusive content!

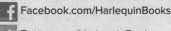 Facebook.com/HarlequinBooks

Twitter.com/HarlequinBooks

Instagram.com/HarlequinBooks

Pinterest.com/HarlequinBooks

ReaderService.com

EXPLORE.

Sign up for the Harlequin e-newsletter and
download a free book from any series at
TryHarlequin.com.

CONNECT.

Join our Harlequin community to share
your thoughts and connect with other
romance readers!
Facebook.com/groups/HarlequinConnection

 **HARLEQUIN**®

**ROMANCE WHEN
YOU NEED IT**

HSOCIAL2018

Reward the book lover in you!

Earn points on your purchase of new Harlequin books from participating retailers.

Turn your points into **FREE BOOKS** of your choice!

Join for FREE today at
www.HarlequinMyRewards.com.

Harlequin My Rewards is a free program (no fees) without any commitments or obligations.